T0062887

A SILENT SHADOW

A SILENT SHADOW

Life is a journey, enjoy it

AVIJIT KUMAR DE

PARTRIDGE

To order additional copies of this book, contact
Partridge India
000 800 10062 62
orders.india@partridgepublishing.com

www.partridgepublishing.com/india

CHAPTERS

Acknowledgement

This book is a fiction inspired by various tales of my life. I am out-and-out writing this book inspired by my colleagues who were so eager to listen to these tales, which I enjoyed sharing with them as well as theirs. I am truly thankful to all of them who wanted this in a form of a book.

I thank my friends, Prasanna Kumar, Harita Kumari, Thara, Sunil, Sowmya, Ranjit, Arthur Sohan, and Murlidhar VM who has been the source of inspiration to me all along. I always wanted to tell my story. It was only when Jaishri said the story is so funny that I should write a book. Hey, did I mention her before? There she is, one of the most amazing women in the world. She lives her life on her terms. As she shared her story with us, to make it short, she is a runaway from her home to marry her college sweetheart, and also had traveled around the world before she had crossed her teens. She is amazing, I must say.

I thank Anju Pruti and Sudhir KS for their valuable insights on storytelling.

As you proceed, you will see how screwed up one can be, if he does not think straight. How miserable it can be when situations go out of hand, or is it let go out of hand? It is for you to find out.

I call this person "the advisor" because he always gave advice to others, even if they wanted it or not. He involved himself to such an extent to solve it, that he screwed up his life completely. This fellow thought that he knew everything. As he always said, there is a solution to every problem, but what about his own? Everyone has to face problems in life at some point or the other, and it always comes in small packages. When it came to him, he adopted the worst possible solution one can ever choose. So, this is my advisor. A word of caution to you, don't follow his advice he makes herein. He could land you in the soup. Let us see what he is doing right now.

The Beginning

Krishna had appeared his standard tenth board exams and was in the eleventh standard. He was in the same school where he studied for all these years, so were his siblings. He had many friends who lived nearby and many of whom were his classmates. These were the fantastic years of his life. He had a perfect childhood growing up. Despite all this, Krishna was unhappy. He wanted to go to a college. College is fun, and he did not want to miss it. Some of his friends had already moved to colleges in other cities. He had tried in few other colleges but was not successful so far. He wondered how to approach his dad.

Krishna walked into the drawing room. He saw his father seated in the sofa reading newspaper.

"Dad, this is a total mess, I don't want to study in this school."

"What's the problem son? You are in eleventh grade now. Complete your Plus-2. These are very crucial years for you."

"Dad, my friends have all gone to good colleges. I also want to go to a college."

"Son, you have not got a seat in any college, have you?"

"Dad, please listen to me, I want to go to a college."

Krishna's father put the newspaper down. Krishna said to himself, this is my last chance; I need to find a good alternative, dad won't say no.

"I want to go to Kolkata."

"So it is now Kolkata!"

"Dad, the colleges there have just reopened and probably admission is going on. Please let me go."

"Son, if you do not get a seat within 15 days, you are coming back, do you understand?"

"Thank you so much. I love you."

"This will be your first time you will travel alone. You should take care of yourself, understood?"

"Yes, dad!"

The following day, he was at the railway station the middle of the night to take a train to Kolkata. He did not have a reservation for this travel. After he had purchased a regular ticket, he stood in the waiting area for the train to arrive. What was this little boy thinking? He was off to college now, but his dad gave him 15 days' time. That's not fair, he thought. How could he get himself admitted in a college in 15 days? He did not even know the names of colleges. He had already experienced the ordeal of getting the prospectus, admission forms, etc. He but had failed to obtain so far, but he desperately wanted to go to a college.

"Only 15 days, dammit! What do I do? Where do I go? Whom do I approach? I will run into trouble if I can't. I have to succeed." He felt dizzy as he thought about what he had left behind. He would miss his childhood friends, his school, and teachers; nevertheless, his parents and siblings. He was also leaving a safe and secured township of Belpahar and had embarked on an 8-hour journey to Kolkata. He heard an announcement, "6002 up Bombay Mail via Nagpur to Howrah arriving on platform number 3."

Krishna quickly picked up his baggage and walked out of the waiting area towards the platform number 3. As he walked over the over-bridge, he could see the headlight of the train approaching fast on the tracks. He ran down the stairs to the platform. The train had already entered the platform and was slowing down. Passengers were running on the platform alongside the train as it slowed down and came to a halt. Passengers pushed each other to make their way into the compartment. The train would halt for only two minutes. Everyone tried to board as fast as possible. Krishna boarded the train in one of the compartments. He saw all the passengers were fast asleep in their berths. Lights were off, dark except for one or two night lamps glowing. It appeared to him like stars at night. At the far end of the compartment, the light was still on. He walked past the entire compartment looking for a vacant berth; he could not find any. He had a heavy baggage on his shoulder and had to drag himself as he walked through. "This bag is heavy. My shoulder hurts." The last berth was vacant.

Krishna put his bag down and sat down and looked out of the window. The whistle blew; the train left the station. It picked up speed quickly and was racing down the tracks. His heart pounded when he thought of the risks he had taken.

The ticket examiner had arrived. "Ticket please." Krishna reached to his pocket and held the ticket in his hand.

"Sir, can I get a berth please?"
"Fifty rupees."

A sleeper berth costs only rupees twenty and no more. The ticket examiner asked for an exorbitant sum of money from him. He reluctantly took out rupees fifty and handed over to the ticket examiner.
"Your berth number is 71."

Krishna is on his way to chase his dream, a young lad from a small town. He has left his school where he could easily complete his twelfth. What was wrong there? Nothing apparently; he was studying in one of the best schools within 100 square miles. Krishna felt he was in jail. He had to wear school dress every day, see the same old faces around, and the same teachers and the strict discipline. He wanted to get out from a small town. He wanted to see the world. He wanted to be a free bird and fly high. He wanted to explore the world.

The train went past a few more stations and had not stopped at any of them. As he opened the shutter of the window, a cool breeze blew in. It was dark outside. He looked out of the window, and the train crossed many villages. Krishna watched the moonless night sky aimlessly deep in his thought about his future. As the time passed, fatigue took over, he yawned and dozed off.

He had reached Howrah Station at around 8 a.m. He had to take a suburban local train to reach his hometown of Hooghly. He knew the route very well. He had been here many times with his parents. The journey is an hour from

Howrah. He went to the ticket counter and purchased a ticket to Hooghly. He had to travel north on a suburban train. He saw the train at the platform number 2 which would take him home. He boarded the train and took a seat. The suburban trains travel at a high speed. They halt at a station for a minute or two. The train stops over at several small towns every few minutes. As the train traveled, it went past the coconut trees, ponds, and lakes, paddy crops, and villages. Krishna could see farmers working in their fields, cranes flying in the sky. The smell of the fertile land of rural Bengal energized him. He had traveled through this route many times in past but this time, he was jubilant to travel independently.

Krishna was trying to figure out which college he should try first. He decided to try his luck at Hooghly Mohsin College. This college was where his father, grandfather, and aunt had studied.

Krishna reached Hooghly. He hired a cycle rickshaw to take him to his home. After a good 30 minutes, he was at the front door of his paternal home. The house was a two-storied building, approximately 75 years old. The main entrance was a large door with 2-inch thick door panel with wooden carvings on it. It also had an arch made of plaster above it with floral designs. The door had a ceramic plate fixed from inside and his grandfather's name engraved on it. It read, "Dr. Jamini Mohan Mitra."

His grandfather was no more. He had passed away many years ago. His uncle's family resided in the house along with his grandmother. He walked up to the door and knocked.

His grandmother opened the door. "Oh My God! Krishna! You have come; so good to see you. Look, who is here!" she acclaimed in astonishment. All his family members came down one by one greeting him on the staircase on his way upstairs. He met with his uncle, aunt, and his cousin brother and two cousin sisters.

"So, what brings you here?" uncle asked.

"I am here to join college," replied Krishna.

"Good news! The colleges are issuing forms now. Check it out tomorrow," replied uncle.

Krishna walked through the huge arched entrance of Hooghly Mohsin College. The gate was wide open as if inviting him. There he could see hundreds of students of his age, many of whom were here with their parents or elders, few others seated in the portico of the classrooms chatting among themselves. He walked up to a person, probably a staff, distributing handouts to students as they came in.

"Where can I get the admission forms?"

"Go to the Main Building, straight ahead."

He walked into a huge archway, an extended part of the Main Building, a grand entrance to the building. As he walked through, the archway led him to two huge doors adjacent to each, the entrance to the Main Building. This building was called Perron's House named after French General Perron who lived in this house, now a college.

As he entered through one of the doors, to his amazement, he saw a huge flight of stairs on the either side reaching to the floor above. The roof was very high, around 25 feet. He noticed cobwebs hanging from the roof and along the walls. He had not seen cobwebs in his school building. He stepped on staircase holding the wooden banister, "Dhum!" a sound of a drum echoed all around. The staircase was a well-carpeted wooden staircase. On each step to the top sounded like the drums of beating retreat of an army parade, welcoming him all the way. He went up the staircase, the sound grew louder and louder and then died out smoothly. At the top, he stood before a large hall, which appeared like a dance floor.

"So, this is the place where damsels danced. Wow! What a treat it might have been!"

He could visualize the bygone era. He saw guests and royalties drinking and merry making seated on the 6-inch mattresses on the floor and some musicians seated at one corner and playing some antique instruments of unknown kind. At the center stage, three dancers sang and performed before the guests.

Suddenly, he realized that he was in the college bustling with activity. He saw students all around busy talking to each other as they passed by. As he walked past the classrooms on either side, he could see a placard, "Administrative Office" at the end of the hall. He walked into the room. He saw staffs were busy collecting forms from applicants.

"Where can I get the forms please?"

"Go to the cash counter over there."

He stood in the queue at the cash counter. After standing for half an hour, he received the application form. The cashier told him that he had to submit the forms by 4 p.m. tomorrow, the last day of receiving forms. Krishna rushed home. He filled up the form and affixed his photograph on it and signed it. Furthermore, he needed a signature of a government official to make it complete. He had to wait for his uncle to return home. After his uncle had come home, he met with him in the bedroom.

"I need a signature of a government official on this form. Where do I get it done?"

"Don't worry son; I will take you to my friend's office tomorrow, relax."

"Oh, I need not worry. I will be able to deposit the form before 4 p.m."

Krishna was very pleased. He had done all that it takes to be in a college of his choice.

The following morning he accompanied his uncle to his friend's office, a high-ranking government official, who put his signature and rubber stamp on it.

"That makes it complete," he said. He went straight to the college and submitted the form. He came to know that the list would be out in seven days.

A week had passed; the list would be out any day. One day, the telephone rang. He picked it up; his uncle had called. "The list is out, go check it out." His heart pounded like a piston of a railway engine. He went to the college and inquired about the list. It was on the main notice board. He ran the entire flight of stairs. The sound of the stairs merged with his heartbeat. He stood for a while in the hall and looked for the notice board. He saw a flock of students gathered around it. He gasped for air to catch a breath. He moved closer to the notice board. As he scanned through the list, his name did not appear in the list. "Oh, God! I have not made it, what shall I do?"

Then a student standing beside him told him of another list for the Morning Section on the notice board at the far end of the administrative office. He rushed towards it. This time, his name appeared on the list. He read it repeatedly to reconfirm. He noted his name in serial number 17 in a list of 65 students. He was very excited. He wanted to dance with joy. He swayed his hands and buttocks on the either side like an African dancer on that spot and threw his fist in the air. "Wow! I have made it."

He went home with a packet of sweets to distribute to his grandma and family members who were eagerly waiting for the good news. He called his uncle at his office and informed him of the news. "Congratulations! I am so happy for you. You are the third generation to carry forth the family tradition of being a student of Hooghly Mohsin College. Call your father to inform him now."

Those were the days when a few homes had subscriber trunk dialing facility, and having a phone itself was a privilege. Krishna rushed to the nearest post office to make a call.
"Trunk call to Belpahar, 06645 please."
"Here is the phone, make your call" handing over the telephone set to Krishna. Krishna called his father at his office.
"May I speak to Mr. Mitra please?"
"Sir, a call from your son," said the speaker. His father came on the line.

"Dad, Krishna here. Dad, I secured a seat in the Morning Section of Hooghly Mohsin College."

"Congratulations son, I am proud of you. When are you coming home?"

"Home! Why dad?"

His father replied, "We have to celebrate. You also have to take your belongings from here to start living there."

"Dad, I will leave tomorrow. I have to be back within a week; the classes will start in 10 days' time." He put back the receiver.

The following day, he went to the college and completed the admission procedure. That night, he took a train journey to Belpahar.

DAY ONE

Krishna came back after ten days as he said he would. The college reopens tomorrow. It will be his first day at college. He was feeling euphoric. He woke up early in the morning. He bathed in the river, the Ganges, which flowed a few meters away from his house. He came home and dressed up in a pair of jeans and a T-shirt. He went to his study table picked up the diary which his father gave him a few days back. He halted before the pooja room to seek the blessing of the Gods and Goddesses. He went down the stairs to his grandma and touched her feet and said, "Grandma, today is my first day at college, I seek your blessing." Grandma blessed him. He said, "Uncle and aunt are asleep. I am leaving now." He took out his new red bike and drove it as fast as he could towards the college gate.

He saw many senior students standing at the college gate. One among them asked to show his college ID. His enthusiasm suddenly melted away like butter put in a hot frying pan. These ragging generals are here at the gate, he murmured. He reached out in his pocket and took out the college ID card and showed it. The senior looked at it and then looked at him. Krishna had a petrified look on his face. "Krishna Mitra, standard 11, right?"

Krishna's voice box suddenly seemed to stop functioning. He cleared his throat and said in a feeble voice. "Yes, sir." Everyone around him laughed.

"Welcome to Hooghly Mohsin College." The senior student handed a rose to him.

"Today is freshers' welcome at the main hall; please be there before 8:30 a.m."

"Phew… saved from being ragged by seniors for now."

At around 8:30 a.m., all students had assembled in the hall and sat on the floor waiting for the event to begin. The program started with the speech by the principal. The principal gave a few words of advice to the new students who had joined this year. He also mentioned about the famous personalities, to name a few, Bankim Chandra Chatterjee, Mrityunjay Sil, Kanailal Dutta who studied in this college over the years. After the principal's speech, a cultural extravaganza began. The seniors of the college gave solo instrumental presentation one after the other. First came the flute, then the violin, and at the end electric steel guitar. Then a fifteen-minute break. A packet of snacks distributed among the students. After the break, Rabindra Sangeet and bhajans were sung by groups of students. The event concluded with a dance performance by senior girls of the college.

The following day, regular classes had begun. His first class was physics on the second floor of the Science Block. Krishna went in search of the classroom. He found it on the second floor as directed. The classroom was like an amphitheater, ten rows of seats, each row a few inches above than the previous. A few students were in the classroom who sat in the last row. The first row was vacant. He entered the classroom and sat on the bench in the first row. After a while, a very handsome boy came and sat next to him. He introduced himself as Sandeep from St. Peter's High School. Everyone knew St. Peter's High School, one of the best schools in the neighborhood. Krishna was from a place 400 miles away, and no one had heard of Belpahar. Krishna had to introduce himself. What could he talk of Belpahar? "I am Krishna Mitra."

"From?" asked Sandeep.

"I am an out-station candidate. I studied in a private school run by the Tata Group of Industries. My father is a senior manager," said Krishna proudly.

"Wow! Tatas! Let us be friends." Sandeep had a firm handshake with Krishna.

Sandeep told Krishna that some of his classmates from St Peter's were here. He would introduce him to all of them. Krishna nodded his head blissfully and waited for the lecture to begin. Then a few more boys came in. They sat in the last two rows leaving benches vacant in between. A flock of girls came in and occupied the rest of the first row seated next to Krishna and Sandeep. Krishna could not figure out why the boys were sitting at the far end of the classroom.

The professor came into the classroom and looked at the class and then proceeded to the dais.

"I am Pramod Bhattacharyya, your lecturer in the Department of Physics. Today, I will start with the first module, Mechanics." The blackboard was large, at least 15x5 feet. He turned and wrote on it in bold letters, FORCE. "What is the definition of force?" He asked.

The class was pin-drop silent. Prof. Bhattacharyya eyes wandered across the rows of students looking for answers. All students sat quietly. Students rarely carried any textbook with them to college. A few students had a Physics book with them today. They have one notebook where they take notes of all lectures they might have attended. Prof. Bhattacharyya had asked a fundamental question, and students were expected to know it, but students kept silent waiting for Prof. Bhattacharyya to pick a student.

Prof. Bhattacharyya called out a student, "You there, in blue shirt, stand up and answer the question?" The boy stood up but was silent for a long time. Prof. Bhattacharyya was very annoyed with the poor response from the class.

"Plus-2 will not be easy, rather very difficult. Now, that you are in the college, you need to study yourselves, and no one will push you around. You should come prepared to the class. If you do not work hard, I am sure most will fail." Prof. Bhattacharyya continued with the class. "Open your book page 53 and start reading from it."

The class went on for 45 minutes. Krishna was busy taking down the notes what Professor Bhattacharyya had been explaining with detailed diagrams that he drew on the blackboard. He had mastered the art of taking notes from the lectures in his schooldays. He was thankful to his class teacher, Mr. Verma, who had insisted on getting used to taking notes from the teacher's lectures, rather than dictation. The bell rang. The students ran through the corridor, down the staircase out of the Science Block.

As Krishna and Sandeep came out of the Science Block, Sandeep inquired, "Could you follow PB's lecture? Is this a lecture? I could not follow his lecture, but you! You were busy taking notes. What were you writing?"

"I was just taking down his lecture. At home, I will find out the part he covered, that's all *yaar*,"

"Meet with my friends from St Peter's." He introduced Ravi, David, and Manoj to Krishna.

"Hey boys!" a voice heard a few yards from them. Two more joined the group. "I am Joy, and this is James. I am from Darjeeling and James is from Don Bosco."

"Meet Krishna Mitra from…which place you mentioned?" asked Sandeep.

"Belpahar," replied Krishna in a low tone.

"Hey guys, did you notice our class?" said David.

"What is it?" Joy asked inquisitively.

"Those girls from St. Augustine's, they are here. Be careful boys! Keep clear! Don't talk to them," warned David.

"Yeah, dangerous," said Sandeep.

Dangerous! How can that be? He had studied all his life in a co-ed school where boys and girls studied and played together. Girls, his classmates, and they were all good friends all along, and now here is someone who says girls are dangerous wondered Krishna. "Perhaps they are," thought Krishna.

"Do you know them?" asked Krishna.

"Yeah! most of them," replied David.

"Those three girls seated under the tree, Anita Gupta, Indrani Shah, and Parmeet Kaur."

"What about the others?" inquired Krishna.

"Those two, going towards them, that fat girl is Dipti and along with her is Pinky," continued David.

"Birds of a feather flock together," said James.

"Okay, let us go now," said Ravi.

Krishna with his new found friends walked towards the canteen. The canteen roof and walls had patches black smoke fumes which had accumulated over the years. They ordered bread toast with butter and tea. Mr. Shaw was the proprietor of the canteen. He was a male in his mid-40s and looked much older than his stated age. His had gray hair. He was lean, and lanky and always had a "*beedi*" in his mouth, smoking all the time. He doubled up as a cook of the canteen.

As the days passed, the group became even larger as a few more students joined in the hearty conversation. They spent their time during the breaks in the boy's common room or played sports and games, mostly playing table tennis, football, and cricket. Often, they would bunk class to watch movies in the local theaters. The attendance in the class was significantly low, only thirty of them used to attend classes regularly.

UNDERGROUND

At college, students have liberty to do whatever they desire. Often, with this new found liberty, students engage in fruitless activities, but some enjoy it, so did Krishna. The weekly schedule at college had a few free periods. At these times, students were either in the canteen or the common room playing table tennis or some board games.

Krishna was in the canteen with his friends. They ordered bread toast, scrambled eggs, and tea, which they shared among themselves. Mr. Shaw, the cook, proudly presented it to them. Students used to order the same menu most of the time. Mr. Shaw thought he was the best chef in the world as he always received repeat orders. He served it with pride. Students with little pocket money relished it.

Krishna spoke, "Guys, heard of a tunnel in the college campus."

"Never heard of it," remarked Joy.

"Who told you about it?" inquired Sandeep.

"Nothing like that," remarked James.

"It exists. My father and grandfather studied in this college," replied Krishna.

"Let's find out," said Joy.

"Are you guys coming with me?" asked Krishna.

So, they set out looking for the tunnel.

"Where could the tunnel be?" inquired James.

"Since the main building is the oldest part of the college, let us start from there," replied Krishna.

"Yeah! There is room near the principal's cabin. We should check it out," remarked Joy.

They entered the Main Building and walked through the hall into the corridor past the principal's cabin. They looked around to check to see if anyone had noticed them. They entered into a narrow passage leading to one end of the building into a small room, dark even in broad daylight. A small ventilator at the top, the only source of light, and a beam of sunlight touched the floor. They walked into the room, and there they found a spiral staircase made of cast iron leading to the underground. The staircase was completely dark, and a large amount of dust had accumulated as nobody had stepped in for years.

"This must be the way," remarked Krishna.

They went down the staircase holding hands with Krishna leading from the front. He found the staircase broken at the last two steps. Krishna jumped down, and dust covered his feet.

"Steady boys, absolutely dark here, cannot see a thing. Does anyone have a match?" inquired Krishna. Joy, a smoker, took out his lighter to show the way. They walked to a large open space underground.

"Where is the tunnel?" inquired James.

"Must be somewhere here," replied Krishna walking ahead.

"Who is down there?" A grumpy voice heard from the top of the staircase.

"What are you people doing there, come back."

A security guard had followed them and came down a few steps behind them. He switched his torch, and the beam of light fell on Krishna's face. They quietly came back following him their way up.

"Straight to the principal's office," said the security guard.

"Sir, these students were in the old staircase down there," said the security guard.

"Boys, which class?" asked the principal

"Standard 11, sir," replied Sandeep.

"Why weren't you in class?"

"Free period," replied Joy.

"Free period! What were you doing in the down there in the abandoned godown? There are snakes! Don't you know this area is out of bounds for students?"

"I told you tunnel did not exist," murmured James.

"Keep quiet," said Sandeep.

"Sir, Krishna's idea," said James.

"Idea! What idea?" asked the principal.

"We were looking for the tunnel," replied Joy.

"Tunnel?" exclaimed the principal.

"Sir, I told him tunnel did not exist," said James.

The principal leaned back on his push back chair, smiled, and said, "Well, ah!.... tunnel existed long ago, the government had sealed it off. I don't want you people wasting time on such trivial matters. Now, go to the class."

"Sorry, sir." All of them said together.

"Thank you, sir" replied Krishna and left the principal's cabin with his friends.

They went straight to the canteen. Ravi could not find them around and was waiting for them.

"Where were you guys?" questioned Ravi.

"The principal called us," replied Joy.

"What is the matter?" inquired Ravi.

"Nothing much, he wanted to know about our preparation for the upcoming exams," replied Krishna evading the truth.

"I was looking for you," said Ravi pulling Krishna aside.

"What is it?"

"You know Diana, don't you?"

"Diana! Who is she?" remarked Krishna.

"Indrani *yaar*!"

"Why do you call her Diana?"

"Didn't you notice she has a hairstyle, like that of Princess Diana of Wales?"

"What can I do for you?"

"The other day I saw you talking to her, so I thought you might be able to help me" continued Ravi, "I have a huge crush on her."

"Oh, she is leaving now," said Krishna as he saw her from the canteen window walking out of the main gate.

"Pick a red rose from the flower shop and give it to her and say I love you. Take my bike and go now" throwing the keys towards him.

"Where did Ravi go?" asked Joy.

"After Indrani" replied Krishna.

They waited at the canteen for about 20 minutes. Ravi came back driving the bike at a high speed. His eyes wide open and mouth gasping for air as if hit by a thunderbolt.

"What happened?" inquired Joy.

"She took it and said I love you too. I had been waiting to hear it from you for such a long time," mentioned Ravi.

"You are fabulous, Krishna," remarked Ravi and hugged Krishna.

"Every problem has a solution," said Krishna.

"You are a guru. Henceforth, we will call you Guruji" remarked Joy.

"As you wish" Krishna replied. "I am getting late, yaar! Got to go home."

"Wait Krishna! Need to celebrate" ordering tea, but this time a special treat; *dal-puri* and *ghugni*. *Dal-puri* and *ghugni* are Bengali recipes. *Dal-puri* is made from skinless green gram boiled until soft and then mashed and mixed with spices and put in as stuffing in a flatbread fried in oil. *Ghugni* is gravy made from boiled dried peas mixed with exotic spices.

Krishna was getting ready to get back home. He bid goodbye to his friends and left the canteen. As he walked towards his bike, he could see Dipti right before him. She was running towards him, approaching fast, appeared like a wild tusker charging at him flapping her ears, straight from the African Safari. Her open hair flew in the air like the ears of an elephant.

"Krishna,...wait," she said. Krishna wondered what was her intention? A voice from inside said, "Run, Krishna, run." Krishna turned back and was about to run; he heard, "Don't run away Krishna! I cannot run so fast. Please wait."

Krishna froze there and then. Dipti came up to Krishna and asked, "Can you give your diary for a day? I want to copy PB's notes." He reluctantly gave the diary to her. She said, "Actually, not me, Parmeet wants it."
"That's okay," replied Krishna.

Dipti took the diary in her hand, turned toward the girls seated under the tree. She waved Krishna's diary vigorously in the air and said, "Got it, girls."

His father had given him this diary, priceless possession. The diary had a picture of Lord Krishna and his eternal consort, Radha Rani on it. He used to take this diary to the college every day. He used it to take notes of all the lecture sessions he attended. If he lost this, it would be a major setback to his studies. Krishna wondered did she want PB's notes or was it something else. "Gone! There goes my diary forever. The most valuable possession, gone! What if she does not return?" David had warned him of them before. He was skeptical about the girls and their intentions.

A PERFECT 10

The loss of the diary was so worrisome to Krishna that he could hardly get good sleep that night. He wondered how to get his diary back. Should he speak to his friends? Should he try getting it back himself? What to say to his friends? What assistance he could seek from them? Sandeep would not help. He assumed that he already lost his diary, and so started to look for ways and means to adapt without it. He realized that he had not made notes at home for some time now. If he had done it, a copy of the lectures would have been up-to-date in his home notebook. Flipping the pages, he found out that he has not made fresh notes on to his notebook for the past two weeks, pretty lazy I must say. What the hell have I been doing these days? The semester exams are just ahead and no time left. He made up his mind to get his diary back some way or the other.

Krishna was in the college looking for Dipti; she was not around. He asked all his friends about Dipti's whereabouts. No one had seen her of late. She was not in the class either. "I should speak to Indrani, she was with her yesterday," thought Krishna. He went up to Indrani and inquired about his diary. Indrani replied, "Yes, I have seen your diary. Parmeet has it now."
"Oh! It did not strike me before," remarked Krishna.

"Where is Parmeet?

"There she comes," replied Indrani and Parmeet walked up to them.

"Hi! Krishna."

"Hi! You have my diary. Please give it back to me."

"What's the hurry?"

"I want it now."

"Hold on."

She sat next to Indrani, opened her handbag and peeped into it and took out the diary. "Here, I got it," she said and handed over the diary to Krishna. Krishna took the diary and flipped through the pages. He noticed a peacock feather and a small card in between the pages. He picked up the card along with came the peacock feather glued to it. The card had a small drawing of Mickey Mouse on it. He opened the card, it read:

"To Krishna,

Thank you

From Paro.

"Wow! Nice card. Thanks!" said Krishna.

"Your name is Paro or Parmeet?"

"Friends call me Paro."

"*Devdas ka Paro*?" asked Krishna in an inquisitive tone and smile on his face.

"No, just Paro."

"Why this peacock feather?" holding the card in his hand.

"Krishna is incomplete without his peacock feather."

"Oh! Krishna has Gopis too. I don't have any," remarked Krishna.

"Many around you, can't you see?" Paro burst into laughter. She held Krishna's hand and pulled him next to her and said, "Come, sit here." Krishna obliged.

"Krishna, you live with your parents?"

"No, I am at my grandfather's house with my uncle and his family. My parents are in Orissa. My father is working there."

"Belpahar."

"How do you know that?"

"Your address is in your diary. I am also away from my parents living with my elder brother. He works in Dunlop."

"Don't you miss your family?"

"Yes."

"I miss my parents. We are from Bhatinda, Punjab. My parents reside there. I am here at my brother's place."

Parmeet opened up to Krishna telling him more about herself. She had come here at an early age and joined St. Augustine School in standard IV. She lives with her brother. She has been pursuing her education here ever since. She also mentioned about her sister-in-law, whom she calls "Bhabhiji," a loving and caring person. She has a niece who studies in standard VIII at St. Augustine's.

"So, what do you want to be?" inquired Paro.

"I will be a doctor like my grandfather, I guess."

"Family tradition, right?"

"No, my father is an engineer, but my grandfather and great grandfather were doctors."

"I want to be a nurse. There are good job opportunities in the UK for nurses. Maybe one day I will go there."

"Have you met Pinky?"

"No" replied Krishna.

"Her father is Home Minister."

"Oh! He works from home?" Krishna smiled in anticipation.

"It's not funny. Haven't you heard of our Home Minister, Sukumar Ghosh? He is her father."

"Oh! That goon! Got to be careful. He must have spies all around here." Krishna looked around for unfamiliar faces.

"She is not what you think of her. Come, meet her."

She called out, "Pinky, can you come here please."

"Meet Krishna. He is not one of those St. Peter's boys. He is from Belpahar."

Krishna could understand these girls too did not have a good opinion of his friends either.

"Hi! Krishna," said Pinky and sat beside Krishna.

"I was telling him about your father," mentioned Paro.

"Yeah! People fear him, but my dad is a good person. He has done great service for the poor. He built many hospitals and schools in the villages, but still public doesn't understand him. It happens with politicians. I have learned to live with it."

"Come to my house this weekend," mentioned Pinky.

Krishna remained seated there thought for a while, "I will go to a politician's house. No, not me! The Home Minister's residence! No, I won't go, I hate politicians."

Krishna saw Sandeep, Ravi, and David coming towards him. Sandeep said, "There he is."

"What is this Krishna? You are sitting here with the girls, and we were looking for you in the entire college," said David bewildered and confused.

"What's up guys?" Krishna asked.

"We have to play a match with our seniors, second-year science tomorrow, and you are sitting here. Come let us go for a net practice."

"Ravi," called Indrani. Ravi went up to her.

"Meet me after an hour. I will be there; you know where. Don't forget. It is important."

"Okay, I will," replied Ravi.

He pulled Krishna's hand and dragged him along with the others.

"Bye! Paro," said Krishna and walked out with his friends.

"Who is Paro?" inquired David.

"Parmeet."

"So, she is Paro, hmm! What's up?" inquired Sandeep.

"Nothing, she had my diary."

"You gave your diary to her!" remarked David.

"She wanted my notes. Forget it, I got it back," replied Krishna.

Krishna and his friends went to the cricket ground and had their practice session. Ravi did leave within an hour that day. The match with second-year science next day was a close finish. They won the game by just two runs. It was a superb batting display by Joy, the skipper, with a good partnership with David.

Few days had passed, one day; Manoj came up to Krishna and said, "Guruji, you have solutions for all problems, don't you? You seem to figure it out easily. Your help brought Ravi and Indrani together. Can you help me?"

"Well! who is the lucky girl?" Krishna asked.

"Hey! Don't tell it to anybody, promise me."

"Okay, I won't."

"She knows you well."

"Don't tell me, Pinky! She is minister's daughter. Do you understand?" Krishna could not think of anyone else. This boy must be crazy. No doubt Pinky was the most attractive girl in the class, and naturally many boys could get attracted towards her.

Manoj replied, "No! not Pinky, Anita is my heartthrob."

"So, why do you think I can help you?"

"Well, you are in good terms with St. Augustine's girls. Parmeet is your friend and Anita is a friend of Parmeet, so perhaps you can talk to her."

"Manoj, why don't you express your feelings to Anita?"

"I am afraid that I may mess up. Please talk to her on my behalf. Do some of your magic."

"Okay! I will give it a try. Give me some time. I will speak to Anita."

"Please, make it fast," requested Manoj.

Krishna could not find time to speak to Anita the same day as she kept herself busy attending all lecture sessions. The exams were also just in few days' time. The following day, Krishna found Anita in the library. She was alone at this time busy taking notes from a chemistry book she had borrowed from the library. Krishna went up to her and sat next to her.

"Hi! Anita."

Anita raised her head and smiled. "Hi! Krishna! You are here, and Paro was looking for you. She was here a moment ago. She just left."

"I came to meet you."

"What is it?"

"What is your opinion about the St Peter's boys?"

"Those are a bunch of jokers." Krishna was taken aback. He did not expect such a statement from Anita.

"They are my friends! our classmates!" Krishna looked at Anita in astonishment. He said, "That's the opinion you hold about my friends and me."

"No, you are different."

"How is that?"

"We know these boys for a long time." She went back to her notebook and continued to take notes from the library book.

"Hold on, have you spoken to any of them recently?"

"No, not here in college, about a year or two ago."

"Well, your opinion is biased. You have not met Manoj recently. You should speak to him. He is a good friend. He told me he is deeply in love with you. He will go crazy if you don't speak to him."

"Oh, really? Please don't cajole me, Krishna!"

"I know you two are made for each other. I spoke to Paro. She also agrees you both could make a good couple."

"She would have told me before."

"I told her to hold on until I talked to you."

She was silent for a while and then shut her notebook and picked up the chemistry book and notebook from the table and stood up. She turned towards Krishna and said, "I will think about it." She deposited the book in the library and walked out. As Krishna watched her leave the library, he said, "Manoj is waiting for you." Krishna could see Anita walk out of the library, and Manoj met up with her as they walked away. Krishna raised his head towards the sky, closed his eyes, and prayed "O God! Please do your magic on them."

After some time, Manoj, James, Ravi, and Sandeep were at the library door waving at Krishna and asking him to come out of the library. Krishna returned the book he had taken and left the library. Manoj hugged Krishna and said, *"Guruji, tera jadoo chal gaya!"* (Your magic has done wonders.)

This is the story how Manoj could express his love to Anita. They are going strong. Ravi and Indrani are also going steady. The boys and girls of the class had jelled well. They sat together, chatted, shared their notes, discussed every lecture session, and prepared for the semester exams. They were friends and worked as a team; Ravi and Indrani; Manoj and Anita; James, Joy, Pinky, Sandeep, Dipti, Parmeet, and Krishna; not to forget David. He was with their group whenever he attended classes. They were always together wherever they went. Krishna and his friends always occupied the first row of lecture session that they attended. When they bunked, the first row used to remain unoccupied. No one sat on those seats. David was irregular. When he came to college, he used to spend most of his time in the playground rather than the classroom. He was a good sportsman, and played all games well, including cricket, football, and basketball. He always had a place in the college team, so most of the time he was out playing for the college.

The Minister's Daughter

Pinky was the most beautiful girl in the class. She was a beauty with substance. Friends were delighted to be with her. Everybody wanted her company and to be her friend was obviously a privilege. She not only had beautiful looks, but also had a golden heart. She was always smiling. She was approachable to everyone. Everybody was at ease with her, but she was selective about friends. She must have learned the art of communication from her father. Politicians have mastered the skill of communication and leave a superb impression.

Time flies, months had passed, one day Krishna was about to leave the college campus, he heard someone calling "Krishna wait, I want to talk to you." Pinky came up to him.

He went up to her and said "yes Pinky! What's up?"
"I can't talk here…Let's go from here."
"Okay, but where?"
"Restaurant."
"The Little Tibet, do you like Tibetan food?"
"Anything will do. Let's go now."
"I leave first; you will join me later. I will hire a *rick*," said Pinky as she walked towards the college gate. "The Little

Tibet, we meet there." She took an auto-rickshaw ride to the restaurant.

Krishna waited in the college for another 10 minutes and left for The Little Tibet. The restaurant was one and a half miles from the college at a place far away from the maddening crowd, in a small street next to the river Ganges. On reaching the restaurant, Krishna found Pinky waiting outside. They entered the restaurant and went to the first floor. The first floor was the most attractive place to be. Tables were next to the large glass windows overlooking the Ganges. They could see boats sailing in the river. Krishna took a table next to the window and pushed open the glass window. A cool breeze from the river end blew in, a heavenly experience.

"Why did you call me here?"

"I will let you know. First, let us order something." Krishna called the waiter and ordered for two plates of fried momo and Coke.

"What is your opinion about Paro?"

"She is a good friend."

"Just a good friend?"

"Did you call me here for this?" Krishna was bewildered with her question.

"But, Paro…."

"What is it?" Krishna wanted to know more from Pinky.

"Nothing. Forget it. I called you here because I am depressed."

"Why? What happened?"

"Why do your friends call you Guruji, Krishna?"

"There is a story behind all this. I will tell you some other day" avoiding the question.

"I have a gut feeling I know it," she remarked. She continued, "I don't have good friends with whom I can talk freely. You care about others feeling, so I thought I could speak to you."

Pinky spoke in a soft, low tone voice and was teary eyed. A drop of tear from her left eye rolled down the cheek. She reached out to her handbag for a handkerchief and wiped her tears.

"My father is very sick. He is in the hospital."

Krishna was stunned hearing this news. He had a mixed feeling and could not react to it. Wasn't this the person who has said "Give me your vote, I will open a hospital in your village. If you don't, there will be a hospital in every household in the village." The terror campaign was the way to winning elections in his hay days, and now, he is in the hospital. Controlling his thoughts, Krishna asked, "Why? What happened to him?"

"The doctors say his liver is in a pretty bad shape. He requires a liver transplant, and moreover his heart is not stable right now. He is in the ICU."

"So, Pinky's father is suffering from liver cirrhosis, he must have been drinking too much!" thought Krishna.

"Have you asked for a specialist opinion?" asked Krishna.

"Yes, Dr. Nagesh Katyal from Delhi has been consulted."

"I am so sorry to know about your dad's ill health."

"He is not improving at all."

"I am afraid, I may not be able to see him again," continued Pinky.

"Why do you think so?"

"You know, they will not let him live. They will kill him" saying these words, she started crying even more loudly.

"Don't cry. He will get well soon." Krishna handed the glass of water to her.

"Who wants him dead?" asked Krishna.

"Chief Minister."

"What!, the Chief Minister!"

She was now crying like a small baby, and her eyes became red and swollen. Krishna was taken by surprise. Krishna could not think this was happening. He did not know how to comfort her in this situation. He could not think why his party men would want him dead. This is politics; it has its rules. The rule is, there is no rule. Everyone wants to take advantage of other's weakness to go up the ladder or go even to the extent of eliminating anyone coming in the way.

They were in the restaurant for half an hour. She had stopped weeping, but held Krishna's hand tightly and Krishna comforting her. "I want to go home" Pinky in a somber tone. They walked out of The Little Tibet and Krishna dropped her home. Krishna left her at the gate of her house. He did not enter her house even though she requested him multiple times. Krishna thought this is not a good time to visit her home at this hour.

THE D-DAY

The semester exams were just over; only a few scheduled classes held. Krishna used to hang around with his friends, having fun in the college. They often bunked classes and went to the theaters to watch a movie. Krishna always used to move in a group, Wherever they went, they went together, either to a movie or a restaurant. Krishna had this routine for the past one week but often missed Pinky. As you know, her father was in the hospital, and she used to visit him every day. She sometimes came to the college to attend classes but left early during the day.

One such fine day, college election notice was put up. Students were very excited. The first-hand experience of an election for Krishna. All political parties became very active. Many local leaders came into the college and gave speeches. Krishna hardly paid any attention to those speeches. Krishna noticed that the class strength was almost full for every lecture session. All the students used to attend the classes including the hostel boys, who otherwise were very irregular.

The college has two hostels, and a few classmates stayed at each hostel. The daily chit-chat and discussions had shifted from studies to politics. Joy was very much aware of politics.

He often explained the ideologies of all political parties and their affiliates. Krishna was not interested in politics, so he did not participate in their discussion. He would simply sit there and listen to them. Krishna knew nothing about college union and its elections.

The students of each class had to elect a class representative who would be a member of the college union representing the class. Upon completion of the election, a meeting of these members conducted to elect their President, Secretary, and other office bearers. Thus a college union formed. The list of office-bearers of college union is handed over to the management of the college. More or less like any election in the country. A political party used to support a candidate and thus a party would bear all expenses for the campaign. The political party that had the most number of members in the union would control over the college union and thereby the college.

One of those days, Krishna was with his classmates in a classroom on the second floor of the Science Block waiting for the lecturer to arrive. The head of the Department of Chemistry, Professor Ghosh came in. He was surprised to see a large number of students in the class.
"I see many new faces. Are you all from this class?"

A loud reply came from the class, "Yes, sir."

He opened the attendance register and looked at it and said, "Sixty-five students, it seems full strength today."

He took the attendance of the class calling out roll numbers which went on for two to three minutes. He came at the end of the dais and said, "As I see most of you have come today, I am going to introduce a new module today. We will begin with organic chemistry."

Saying this, he turned back and walked three steps to the blackboard to write on it. Someone was at the door.

"Excuse me, sir," Professor Ghosh turned towards the door and said "Yes." The person walked in and along with him came few more boys.

"The elections are around, and we need to speak to the students," said the man. Professor Ghosh said, "Okay, carry on" and left the classroom.

The person took to the dais. He was a tall, thin-appearing gentleman with a full-grown beard and mustache. His hair was rather thin, looked like crow's nest with a bunch of gray hair. He introduced himself the final year student and secretary of a political party. He did not appear so; he looked much older. Krishna wondered how long he must be studying in this college. It must have been more than 8 to 10 years from now when he might have joined this college. "Oh, God! I have to listen to his boring lecture and the chemistry class has gone for a toss."

The leader was a minute or two into his speech, to his utter surprise, Krishna saw Joy stand up, and walked out of the classroom. "He has guts man!" thought Krishna. Within a minute, David followed the suit. Subsequently, few more students from the last row left the classroom. Krishna seated in the first row. He could not muster the courage to walk out right away. He was undecided what to do. After a while, he decided to go. He said to Paro seated beside him, "let's go." She stood up and along with came the entire first row. Within in two to three minutes, all students had left the classroom. Krishna and his friends laughed it out. It made him wonder what an insult it must have been to the party leader as he could not complete his speech. "This might have been a very disappointing experience for our political party secretary friend," said Krishna to his friends. Krishna realized the strength and unity that he had among his classmates.

The following day at the college, Krishna was among friends seated under a tree. Joy came up to him with another senior student and said, "He is Anirban. He is the current secretary of the college union. We want you to represent the class, please sign this application form." Krishna was surprised to hear this. Many students were interested in politics and political parties. He did not understand why Joy was asking him to contest elections.

"No! I will not sign. I do not understand politics," said Krishna.

He wondered why Joy was coaxing him to join politics. Krishna questioned Anirban, "Why me?"

Joy explained, "Listen, we need a candidate from our class, someone has to contest this election. After extensive discussion on who should it be, we decided on you, so sign this form, we will take care of the rest."

"I don't want to be a political leader giving speeches," remarked Krishna.

"You don't have to" remarked Anirban. "This is a college election. You are only going to represent your class. Your classmates are going to vote for you."

Krishna was not comfortable with it and did not agree. He was not convinced. James sat with Krishna and explained to him in more detail. "You are popular among the boys as well as the girls in the class. We are here ten to fifteen of us. We will vote for you. You are in good terms with another fifteen, so that makes thirty, don't forget the hostel boys, five more. I have already talked to them. The rest we will catch up in a day or two. Can't you see you have already won the election? Come on don't be a spoilsport, contest this election."

All his friends had gathered around Krishna listening to James.
"We call you Guruji. You should represent our class," said Ravi.

Paro and Pinky joined them.
"We will vote for you, and we will ask the other girls too," said Paro.
"Don't think, sign it!" said Pinky.

Difficult for Krishna to go against the wishes of Pinky and Paro. Krishna did sign the form. A loud roar heard as Krishna handed over the form to James as if someone has conquered the Mount Everest. James handed over the form to Anirban, who then left to deposit it. James and Joy hugged Krishna and shook hands. Pinky and Paro wished him best of luck. Rest of his friends followed suit.

James was with Krishna the whole day. He had the list of students of the class and was preparing a strategy to approach each one of them. They met with most of the classmates that day and informed them about Krishna's candidature. At the end of the day, James found out that he had to reach out to ten more classmates who were not in the college. Krishna received information that another girl had filed her papers with the influence of another political party. James said, "We will give her a tough contest. You do not worry Krishna." A very tiresome day for Krishna walking around the whole college multiple times. Krishna left home for the day.

The subsequent day, James brought in the rest of the classmates to meet with Krishna. Krishna requested them to vote for him. All his friends rallied around him throughout the day. James ensured that all his classmates stayed together the whole day.

The Election Day had arrived. Krishna was on his way to the college. Police personnel stationed at the main gate, but not inside the campus. They checked IDs of the students and only then let them in. This election was Krishna's first. He was also contesting the election. He was very excited. Krishna had not attained the age eligibility for voting in country's election, so this was going to be his first hands-on experience of a new kind. Over and above this, he was contesting for it. He was pretty nervous. He gathered courage and went to the information desk put up for the students. Joy and James were already here. James said, "You are late by fifteen minutes. Hurry up, let us go to the class. I will explain to you what to do on our way."

Krishna looked around. The college had a festive look. Party banners and posters all around and party flags fluttering in the air. All students were in festive mood. Students came in dressed in their best to the college.

As they walked towards the Science Block, James said "Be at the door, check every student's ID when they come in. Don't let anyone without it. ID is a must to vote." Krishna did as told. His classmates arrived one by one in the classroom. They smiled at him and wished him luck. His group of fifteen friends sat in the first row as usual. The other students turned up soon. Krishna was very appreciative of Pinky. She was there despite her father's illness.

After a while, he saw Prof. Ghosh coming towards the class. Krishna went and sat in his seat. Prof. Ghosh came in and took the dais and said, "Good morning students." The students responded in chorus "Good morning sir."
"Those of you who are not students of this class; please leave the room." Two party workers left the classroom immediately. Prof. Ghosh closed the door. Prof. Ghosh then introduced the process to students as they were first-time voters, "You need to show you ID card to get your voting slip. Go to the covered area right there, a stamp and an inkpad kept there, use the stamp to cast your vote. Fold the slip as I demonstrate here and put it in the ballot box and then leave the classroom."

He further explained the case of a canceled vote and advised to be careful while voting. The voting began and in next half an hour the voting was over. All the students had left the classroom. Prof. Ghosh took then took the ballot box and left the classroom. "There goes my fate in the hands of Prof. Ghosh," said Krishna.

The counting of ballots was held the following day. Krishna arrived in the college, in the morning itself. By afternoon, the counting had begun. Information flowed that the counting had started from the senior most classes. He was in the junior most class and a fresher. It would take some more time to finish. Krishna was very nervous and quiet now. He sat alone in the common room and was not talking to anybody. His friends kept on informing him of the results of various classes, as to who won and by how many votes.

By evening 4 p.m., James came running up to Krishna and said, "Guruji, You have won. They have just finished counting." James, Ravi, Joy, and Sandeep all cuddling together, jumping in joy. It took some time for Krishna to realize and then he started jumping too.

James said, "Do you know the result, the total number of votes 64, absent 1, and 62 is to 2. This has broken the 20-year record of anyone winning by such a huge margin." Krishna was shocked to hear that. James continued, "I am going to nail that bastard, who did not vote for you. I know, he is her lover."
"How do you know he is the guy?" asked Krishna.

Joy remarked, "I always doubted him. I was marking him always. He always avoided me." Forget it," said Krishna, "We have won the election."

Krishna's friends picked him up and tossed him up in the air. He landed in their safe hands. The merrymaking continued for some time. After that, some students brought colored fragrance powder used in the festival of Holi. James with red at one side and Joy with green on the other, they splashed the colors on him and his face. Krishna was looking like a joker half red and half green. His white shirt looked like a tricolor flag.

Amidst the celebration, the inevitable news of Pinky's father came in. The doctors could not save him. He lost the battle against his disease. The news spread throughout the college. Everybody stopped their celebrations there and then. James said, "We have to go to Pinky's house." Everybody agreed with James.

"I cannot go with all this color over me," remarked Krishna. "Rush to the washroom, come back soon. We are waiting for you."

Krishna cleaned himself up and came back to his friends and got ready to leave for Pinky's residence.

"Where are you going Krishna?" inquired Joy.

"I am going to get my bike," replied Krishna.

"Let your bike be here. A Jeep is waiting for us."

"Jeep? Where did you get that?"

"We had planned a victory parade for you, but now forget it. You better start getting used to these things now that you are famous," remarked Joy.

Within next few minutes, the merry making by students and party workers had abruptly come to a halt. The college had a deserted look. As they drove past various shopping places, markets, and theaters of the town, most of them had downed their shutters; others were closing down, people rushing back to their homes. A serious situation indeed Krishna said to himself. They finally reached Pinky's residence. He saw a few party workers standing near the front gate of her house. Krishna came to know that the all family members were at the bedside when he passed away and that they were on their way from the hospital. They would be here by next 20 minutes. They waited there for Pinky's family to arrive. A huge crowd had now assembled around her house. Krishna introduced himself as Pinky's classmate and was let in, and a received warm response from the party workers gathered there.

After thirty minutes, Pinky returned with rest of the family with her departed father in the carriage. Krishna and his friends were with her by her side at this time of grief, the most difficult time of her life. Krishna and all his friends stayed back for her father's last journey to the heavenly abode.

This day was of both happiness and sorrow. Life is like that. Sometimes moments of happiness and at other times moments of grief. One has to learn to accept both as they come. A moment of truth for Krishna. He went back home with mixed feeling. He was unsure of this day would go down the pages of history; a good day or a bad day; surely, very important day of his life. His life had changed that

It is Spring

The cold winter months were over. Thick fog over the Ganges had cleared. Dry leaves from the large trees all over the college campus were lying on the pathways. New leaves had sprouted in the trees and flowers blossomed spreading their fragrance all over the campus. The most attractive spot for the students was the bathing ghat. The Ganges flows right along the administrative building. As one takes the narrow pathway leading to the back of the building, large trees with their branches spread across covers the entire area. The bathing ghat is just a few yards away. A large flight of stairs made of red brick and mortar leads into the river. At the banks of the Ganges is a large banyan tree with the fresh roots swaying in the air just a foot above the ground. Many species of birds had built their nests on the banyan tree. In the evening, as the sun sets over the river, birds chirping in the trees, coming back to their nests remind one that it is time to go home.

If this place was not to be college, then it would be an ideal place to build a heritage hotel. This is a very scenic place, a perfect place amidst the riverside. Whatever it could have been, a matter of debate. The owner of this property was a prominent philanthropist in Bengal. He wanted an education institution. Thus the institution is named after him. If only he knew the better usage of such a beautiful scenic place, in such a scenario, the college would not exist. Furthermore, on my recent visit to the college campus I was devastated to see a huge wall erected at the bathing ghat and could not find the banyan tree beside the bathing ghat. It is probably axed. I don't understand why it was cut down.

The place was where couples often met in the evening. It reminded Krishna of Ravi and Indrani. It was a lover's point. Why just them, most of the couples used to spend their evening here. This place is safe. It happens to be on the campus, so no outsiders to intrude upon their space. No one from the outside world would know about their relationships as this place was beyond the reach of anyone other than the students of the college, thus a closely guarded secret. During the daytime, many student groups occupy the steps of the bathing ghat chit-chatting and leisurely spending their time together.

One such day Krishna was alone seated at one of the steps of the bathing ghat under the shade of the banyan tree, in a quiet and pensive mood. God knows what was going on in his mind. Something was worrying him. There are times when one suddenly experiences lows and knows not why. Perhaps, he was missing his family. It had been eight months since he left Belpahar. He picked up a few pebbles in his hand and threw a pebble into the river; small waves splashed onto the banks of the ghat.

Paro came looking for him to the bathing ghat. She tapped on his back and said, "Krishna, I was here for more than a minute now, and you did not notice me. What are you doing here all alone?"

"Nothing," replied Krishna.

"Come let us go to Botany class."

"No, I don't want to go to the class," replied Krishna throwing another pebble into the river.

"What is the matter?" she asked and sat beside him.

Krishna was quiet with his head down staring at the waves.

"Krishna, turn toward me. Hey! Tell me what is the matter?" raising his chin with her hand towards her.

"I don't know. I am not feeling good," replied Krishna.

"Is it that you are missing your parents?" she asked.

"Perhaps," replied Krishna.

"You are feeling homesick. Aren't you? You are! I know, it happens, I also felt the same sometimes. Come on, cheer up. Let's go to the class."

"No, I won't, you go," replied Krishna.

"I see, well, I am also not going. Here I am with you." She put her handbag down and sat beside him. "What a beautiful day. The sky is clear and blue. Feel the air around you. Take a deep breath."

Krishna looked at her.

"Come on, take a deep breath like this." She demonstrated it to Krishna. Krishna took a deep breath.

"Now, exhale slowly." Krishna obliged.

"Good! just one more time." They repeated the breathing exercise one more time.

"There you are! Aren't you feeling better?"

"Yeah! I am feeling good."

"See it works."

"You know some magic or what?"

"Do you think only you can do magic and no one else."

"Aha, I understand where it is coming from."

"Your stories of Ravi and Manoj are all over the college."

"Oh! That was just a favor to my friends."

"Oh! I see," saying this she removed her sandals.

"What are you doing?"

"I'm going to the river."

She went down the few steps of the ghat. She was into the water at the last step and the waves splashed her feet.

"Wow! The water is very cold. Come down here."

"Yes, I know water will be cold at this time of the day."

"Where in the world can you enjoy mother nature like this? Open your shoes and come down, Krishna."

Krishna could not resist the temptation of the river Ganges. He opened his shoes and went to the river. They went down two to three steps, and they were in ankle-deep in the river. All this made Krishna forget his lows, and he was now enjoying the nature.

Nature is a perfect cure if only one can use it wisely.

"Let us sit in here for a while," requested Paro.

They sat on the steps of the ghat with their feet in water splashing the waves that came on to them talking to each other. A small boat was just passing through near the banks of the river. Krishna stood up and said "Hey! Fisherman, hold on."

The boatman, a young lad of 15, looked at him. Krishna asked, "Brother, are you going fishing?"

"Yes, I am," replied the boy.

"Can we come with you?"

"Okay, hop in," said the fisherman boy and brought his boat to the banks of the river and tied it to the Banyan tree. "Come let's go."

"Where are we going, Krishna?"

"A boat ride," replied Krishna.

They picked up their footwear in one hand and their bags in other and hopped into the boat. The boat started to sail towards the middle of the river. As it moved away from the banks, James came running down the steps.

"Where are you guys going?"

"Fishing," replied Krishna.

Paro laughed and said "Wow! Wonderful to be out here."

"Enjoy the ride guys, bye!" James went back to the college.

"I love you, Krishna."

Krishna replied, "I love you too."

They hugged each other celebrating their new found relationship. The boat sailed to the middle of the river.

ONE YEAR LATER

How quickly the days passed, Krishna could hardly realize. Just a few days ago, he had walked through the gates of the college to seek admission. A year has gone by; he had already appeared for the Class XI final examinations; the results of which were yet to be declared.

He had not seen his family for a year. The summer vacation started. He went back to Belpahar. He was eager to meet his old buddies at school and most importantly spend some time with his family. His schoolmates were his only playmates for all these years. They lived in a small township. Not much goes around here other than the factory of Tata Refractories Ltd. For some, it might be very difficult to visualize such a life, very different from the city except for the people who have lived in a small community township. If you have ever been to such place, you must have noticed rows of look-alike buildings with garages, playground, park, clubs for the community.

Krishna's father was one of the top officials in the company. They lived in a bungalow. As one approaches the bungalow, the boundary wall approximately 100 feet long runs parallel to the road. Looking over the wall at the center is the bungalow with a garden and fruit bearing trees such as mangoes, guava, and many other tropical fruits. A large gate adequate for a car to pass through serves as the entrance to the bungalow. On the left-hand side of the gate is a nameplate with his father's name on it. A pebbled pathway leads to the nine steps up to a sit-out area.

Bungalow has three doors, one on the left, other on the right and one on the center. The right door opens into the drawing room and the left to the guest room. The central door opens to a long passage that has rooms on the either side. On the right side of the passage is the living room, and one the left side the children's room comes first and then the air-conditioned master bedroom. The pathway leads to the dining hall and on the left is the storeroom and next to it at the corner is the kitchen for the lady of the house. At the other end of the dining hall is a door which opens to a courtyard. At the far right of the courtyard is the servant quarter. The bungalow also had a back door at the end of the courtyard mostly used by the servants. There are two rows of such bungalows parallel to each other, about ten in each row.

The families who lived here were like a close-knit family. They share their joy and sorrows with each other and very little to no connection with the outside world. The daily routine of the people here was very predictable. It revolved around the siren of the factory nearby. The way of life around such community runs with a clock precision.

Every morning at 6 a.m., the company siren goes off, time to arise from bed. All activities and daily chores are precisely timed with the siren. To explain this further, just have a look what happens next. Every day at 6:40 a.m., the company car arrives at the door. The officer and a gentleman leave for office. Some officers may take out their private cars from the garage and drive off to the factory. The factory is just a mile away. The lady of the house waves her hand to her husband every day, the way she has been doing all these years. After her husband departs, she shuts the door. The siren goes off again at 7 a.m., the shift starts.

At 8:30 a.m., the door opens again; the children with their school bags on their back and water bottle in their hands come out of the house. Some cycle their way to school while the others walk to school. The school is just a few minutes' walk. The lady of the house then shuts the door and starts off with the household chores.

At 9:15 a.m., a knock at the door, a visitor has arrived. The lady next door comes every day for a conversation with her.

The siren goes off again at noon; it is time for the master of the house to return home. The door opens again; the visitor hurriedly returns to her house. After a while, the children from the school come back. The same car drops the employee home at lunchtime. The lady of the house is very busy. The children depart within next half hour to school again, only to return at 4 p.m.

At 1:45 p.m., the company car arrives again at the gate. It is time for the master of the house to go to office after a 2-hour lunch break. The siren goes off again at 2 p.m. The second shift starts. The lady of the house able to rest a few hours now until the children return.

At 4 p.m., the children are back home and in minutes they are out playing with their friends in the at the nearby park. Some children are out on the school playground for a game of football or cricket.

At 5:30 p.m., the siren goes off. It is time for the master to return. The children are back into the house. The company transport drops the employee at 6 p.m. The master returns home after a day's work at the office.

After a small snack, it is time for recreation. The children are home by or before 6 p.m. It is study time. Some days, the family might go shopping to the cooperative store run by the employees of the factory as it is the only store in the locality. On Sunday evening, they may drop by to a friend's home in the community for a visit.

At 10 p.m., the siren goes off again; the night-shift has started. By this time, all families make sure they get back to their homes, time for dinner. The children go to bed and lights off.

Every household in the community follows the same schedule every day. The only exception is for children who have board exams; the light are on even after 10 p.m.

Krishna was back here in this part of the world. He was very glad to be back with his family. He had missed it very much. After living in Hooghly for a year, his schedule had changed a lot. He did not go to bed before 11:30 p.m. He used to watch television until the transmission was over.

Although his schedule did not match with this way of life here, he adapted to it very quickly as he loved it.

His friends were back. He met his friends in the evening at the officers' club. The club was the most attractive place of all. They played indoor games like badminton, table tennis, carrom board and chess. A full-fledged library and a reading room were at their disposal too. The club also had a swimming pool. The summer is the most enjoyable time out here. The pool filled up only in the summer months. He and his friends used to swim here for hours together. Swimming makes one hungry. No problem, a canteen which served hot *samosas*, cold drinks, chocolates, and few other confectioneries. Just order whatever you want and sign the bill. The bill sent to his father at the end of the month for payment. For entertainment, the club screened movies at the weekends, mostly Hollywood movies. The badminton court converted to a movie theater.

The club hosted parties regularly for the members from time to time. During the festivals of Christmas, New Year, Holi, and Diwali, the place has a special attraction. The lawns are lit up. The badminton court converted to a dance floor. Soothing music from the LP record player. Party games conducted for the ladies and children, and a full-fledged bar for the gentlemen. The party ends with a grand dinner.

At this time of the year, during summer vacation, Krishna could catch up with all. At the end of the vacation, his friends studying in colleges returned to their colleges. The whole of summer vacation he spent here with his parents and siblings.

The summer vacation was over very quickly. The college was to reopen next week. He had to return to Hooghly. He had to prepare for the future ahead of him. It is time to prepare for various competitive examinations, though the preparations do start much earlier, it picks up momentum now. He had to become a doctor and the only way in is entrance examination. Krishna went back to his hometown of Hooghly to continue with his pursuits.

WAS IT A HAT-TRICK?

A few more months had passed since Krishna had his summer vacation. He was busy more than ever. He had to achieve more, and he was working towards it. All science subjects have practical to be conducted in the laboratory of the specific department. The classes would run for two hours each. Most students feared practical class, but Krishna enjoyed doing it. He liked to experiment with chemicals in chemistry and prepare specimen in Biology.

One such a day, Krishna was in the Department of Physiology for his practical class. Professor Dasgupta, his lecturer, was in the laboratory. The topic of the day was the identification of blood cells. Professor Dasgupta demonstrated them how to prepare a slide to identify each blood cell under the microscope.

The slide is made using blood; that too own blood! It is a very simple procedure to prepare. Take a needle of an injection syringe, sterilize it in the hot flame of Bunsen burner and then wait for it to cool down. Use this needle to pinprick your index finger. Blood oozes out within 2 seconds. Just a drop of blood is sufficient to prepare a slide. Use some sterile cotton to stop the blood flow as the blood clots after a while. Put a drop on a clean slide at about $1/3^{rd}$

part of the slide. Use another slide placed at a 45-degree angle at one end and run it over the blood dragging it along its path. A thin film of blood forms over the slide. The slide is then treated with some chemical solution, blood cells take up stains or color and can be easily identified under the microscope.

After Professor Dasgupta had completed his demonstration and asked to do the same, the class fell silent. After every demonstration, the students very enthusiastically do their experiment, but this time, a whole different ballgame; had to use own blood! A difficult proposition altogether. It reminds to what extent little children are afraid of injections. They cry loudly just at the sight of a needle and syringe and want to run away from there. For the students here, they had nowhere to run. They now had to pierce the index finger with the needle.

A student asked Professor Dasgupta, "Sir, I have a question. What if the blood does not come out for the first time?" Professor Dasgupta had replied, "Do it again. Blood will come. You just need a drop."

Krishna was at his desk getting ready for doing the experiment. He lit the Bunsen burner before him. He picked up the needle from the desk and was heating it to sterilize it when Paro approached him and asked, "Are you going to do it?"
"Yeah!" replied Krishna.
"Aren't you afraid?"
"What is there to be afraid of?"
"Blood," replied Paro.

"No, not really."

"I can't tolerate blood. Stop this." Paro pushed the needle away from the Bunsen burner.

"What are you doing to my experiment?"

"What if you die?"

"Are you crazy? I am not going to die!"

"What if you continue to bleed?"

"I am not hemophilic," remarked Krishna.

"Let us go to the lab assistant and ask him to give his blood. Professor Dasgupta will not realize this."

Krishna was utterly surprised. Krishna always found Paro to be a very confident woman. Now, here she is, unable to do a small experiment. She is chicken-hearted thought Krishna.

Within a flash of a second, he pierced the needle in his index finger. The needle went straight in but went too deep. The blood flowed out profusely.

"What have you done?" saying these words Paro took Krishna's index finger in her mouth to stop the bleed.

"I don't want to see you die here. If you want to die, be somewhere else." She put a large piece of sterile cotton and held his finger tight for a few minutes.

Suddenly, a loud thud heard, someone fell on the ground. "What happened?" inquired Professor Dasgupta. "Sir, Paromita fainted" replied James. Everyone rushed to the spot. Krishna saw her lying on the ground a few feet away; her eyes closed. The thought that raced through Krishna's mind, "Oh God! girls are so chicken-hearted, one wicket down." He loved the game of cricket for its uncertainty and excitement.

"Move aside, give way," said Professor Dasgupta. He saw Paromita lying on the floor. He picked her up in his arms and laid her on a bench nearby.

"Will someone get some water please" and asked students to move away from her to allow some fresh air to come in. James went to the tap for a beaker of water. Subsequently, one more thud heard, another girl went down. As James was on his way back with the beaker in his hand, one more girl fainted over him. The water had spilled over his shirt, and the girl was on the ground at his feet. Everybody's attention had moved away from Paromita to these two new casualties. Professor Dasgupta said, "Stop your experiment and leave the lab now. Take a break for 15 to 20 minutes. Go and get some fresh air outside. I don't want more casualties in my class."

While two to three of their classmates stayed back to help Professor Dasgupta nurse his students back to consciousness, all other students proceeded to the bathing ghat. As they walked towards the bathing ghat, Krishna said to Paro, "So, it was a hat-trick!"

"Your classmates were fainting, and you are counting wickets! Stop your sarcastic remarks."

"Yeah! If I did not have the beaker in my hand, I would have stopped her from falling" said James. Paro looked at James surprisingly and then turned towards Krishna for a sympathetic response from him.

"You could be next," remarked Krishna.

Paro hit hard on Krishna's back repeatedly.

"It hurts, Paro."

"Good, you should be punished," remarked Paro.

They all sat at the bathing ghat for half an hour. The girls had recovered by then. All students were back in the laboratory. As the session commenced again, Professor Dasgupta supervised each student turn by turn.

This incident Krishna remembers until this day, such an eventful one.

Operation Sundae

Many days had passed since that incident at the Physiology Lab. The students were now shuttling between theory and practical classes. This time, they were at the Department of Zoology. Zoology is about the animal life; from the single-celled ameba to the largest mammal, the blue whale. Therefore, one comes across snails, cockroaches, toads, fish, guinea pigs, and what not. All that one has to do is to cut open and look inside the body cavity to see how God made them.

The Zoology Department had many animals, such as worms, fish, insects of various kind kept inside cylindrical glass jars. The animal neatly tied to a sheet of glass with a clear liquid inside the jar and permanently sealed from the top. The department had rows of them lined on the shelves of the laboratory.

Krishna and his classmates were in practical class in the laboratory of Zoology Department. That day, the class had a practical session on dissection of a toad. Toads were made available by the department and were inside a large glass jar jumping up and down wanting to escape out. The jar covered with a cover and weight put on it so that they do not jump out.

As they came into the laboratory, their eyes went towards the glass jar. Pinky said, "Today we have to cut open this frog, such a disgusting creature."

"It seems like that," replied Krishna. "It is not a frog but a toad."

Professor Majumdar, a lecturer, was in the laboratory. He was conducting the class. He picked up a chart from the rack and hung it on the wall. That was a diagram of a circulatory system of a toad. He said, "Class, today your will be learning about the dissection of a toad and the circulatory system. I have already covered this in your theory class. Today is your chance to visualize your learning."

He again explained it over through the chart and then asked: "Will someone get me a toad from that jar." James said, "I will," and went to the jar to pick a toad. The toad was alive and kicking. He picked up a toad in his hand and then it suddenly slipped and landed on the floor. It jumped away from James each time he tried to catch it. James after two failed attempts gave up, and said, "Sir, the toad has escaped."

Professor Majumdar looked at James. James was baffled. Professor Majumdar came near the large jar and looked inside. He said, "Call Shankar." Shankar was the lab assistant for the department. He came in. Professor Majumdar was furious at Shankar. "You have not chloroformed the specimens."

Shankar replied, "Oh My God! I forgot. I am sorry."
"You are good for nothing. Now, go and catch that toad."

Shankar went after it. As he attempted to catch the toad by hand, the toad jumped further away from him towards the girls at the corner of the room. The toad somehow knew it was the end of life, giving its last bid to save itself. The girls yelled at the top of their voices and ran away from their desks. Shankar brought a small net with a plastic handle and attempted to catch it. This time, he was successful. He brought the toad back to Professor Majumdar who quickly pinned the specimen on the tray. The toad was now lying on his back with its four extremities pinned on the tray and the belly blowing up like a balloon on each breath. Professor Majumdar said to Shankar, "Will you go now and chloroform the rest of the specimens." Shankar went ahead and poured chloroform in the jar. Professor Majumdar started to demonstrate how to perform the dissection seated beside Krishna. All the students had assembled around them to understand the procedure.

After completing the demonstration, Professor Majumdar said, "Now, get your specimen from Shankar and do it yourself."

All students approached Shankar, who handed over a toad to each of them. They then brought back the toad to their desk and pinned it up on the dissection tray. One should care about the poor toad. It lives in water, so the tray filled with water to make its stay comfortable.

Krishna was in the middle of the experiment when David approached him. He took Krishna aside to a corner of the lab and said, "You got to assist me."
"What type of assistance you want?"
"Assist me to win my bet," showing a small pin in his hand.

Krishna could not understand what his plans were.

"What is the bet?"

"Look at Dipti. She is wearing a saree."

"Yes, …. then what?"

"See those folds around her trunk. It looks like an ice-cream sundae, so yummy. I have to prick her with this pin."

"Who gave you the bet?" asked Krishna.

David pointed his index finger at the entire bunch of boys standing at the far end of the laboratory smiling at him.

"No, I can't do that."

"You don't have to do it. I will. You have to assist me."

"No, I won't."

"You have only to distract her attention. Assist me please," persuaded David. "Watch the fun," he continued.

Krishna thought for a while and still did not agree.

"A treat for you! a Coke!" prompted David.

"Anything for a friend," replied Krishna.

Krishna went to Dipti's desk and engaged her in a conversation. She was in the middle of her dissection, and was so engrossed in it that she hardly noticed David standing just behind her. Suddenly, she shouted, "Ouch!"

"There must be some insect in your saree," Krishna remarked. She stood up and ran outside the laboratory to check it out. David ran towards the boys and did a high-five with them.

"I have won the bet."

After some time, Dipti returned to her desk and continued with her dissection. Indrani and Pinky had noticed David standing beside Krishna with a pin in his hand. They went up to her and told her what they had seen. Dipti stood up and walked to Krishna's desk. He acted busy with his dissection. He could hear the footsteps of Dipti as she came near him. Krishna was worried as he assumed Dipti understood his participation.

Dipti came to Krishna and said, "Do you know, it was David who used a pin on me."
"Oh! Is that true? These St. Peter's boys are nasty," commented Krishna separating himself from his friends.

Until now Dipti does not know that Krishna participated in the plan "Operation Sundae" and hopes she never knows.

THE TRIO

Time and tide wait for none. Krishna was just three months away from his board examination. His preparation is progressing, but not as it should be for the board examination. He had realized that of late.

One such day in the college, he was with Paro in the classroom. She asked, "How is your preparation for the board exams?"

Krishna replied, "I am yet to complete the syllabus."
"Hardly three months to go."
"I will catch up soon," replied Krishna.

Paro suggested that they should begin a joint study and take tutorials to cover up the deficit. Krishna agreed as he would now be able to spend a few more hours with Paro. He was looking for this opportunity for long. Paro had already spoken to Dipti about the joint study and tutorials. She agreed to her proposal provided she was not required to travel a long distance. Therefore, Paro, Dipti, and Krishna teamed up for tutorials. They approached Professor Majumdar and persuaded him to provide tutorials after college hours at Paro's residence. Incidentally, Professor Majumdar lived near her residence, and it was a matter of convenience. Krishna had to travel ten miles to Paro's home for the tutorials. Nevertheless, he could not miss this opportunity to be in the company of Paro and spend a few hours with her.

The following week, the tutorials and joint study had begun. Every week they met at Paro's residence on Mondays, Wednesdays, and Fridays starting around 3:30 p.m. The tutorial was an effective strategy in the preparation for their board examination. Professor Majumdar covered the entire curriculum in a matter of weeks. He conducted tests every week to ensure his students prepared well for their board exams. He had designated Monday as the day he would conduct the test and show the answer scripts on Friday.

The day was a Friday; Krishna reached Paro's residence. The door was wide open. He went inside the house. There was no one to be seen. He called out, "Paro."

Paro replied from her room, "Krishna, you have come."
"Yes, Bhabhiji, and Nimmi not at home. Where are they?"

He realized that Paro was in her room.
"Bhabhiji has gone to school for a parent-teacher meeting. Come to my room" replied Paro.

He walked into Paro's room. Paro could not decide the saree she would like to wear. She stood before the mirror and picked up a saree and laid it on her body, turned back and asked, "What do you think, Krishna? Should I wear this?"
"Saree is heavy, can you manage?" replied Krishna.

"You are right," said Paro and scrambled among the sarees she had laid on the bed. She would wear a saree for the first time. She prefers salwar-kameez.

"Krishna, please select a saree for me," remarked Paro.

Krishna walked up to the bed and moved two sarees aside. He could see a light pink colored saree down below. He pulled out and said, "You can wear this one. It is light in color and light in weight." Paro immediately obliged "Thank you; your choice is good."

Paro turned her back and removed the saree she was wearing. She picked up the pink saree from the bed and opened it up laid it on the floor holding one end in her hand. Krishna could not believe his eyes that Paro could act such a way before him. Paro turned toward Krishna with a smile. She had already tied the saree around her waist. She quickly draped the saree around her left shoulder. She came close to Krishna and asked again, "Tell me how I look?"

Krishna was stunned to see her in a saree. She looked beautiful in a saree. Krishna was at a loss for words and kept staring at her. Paro noticed this and smiled. "Speak up, Krishna." Krishna looked at her from head to toe.

"You are the most beautiful woman in the world," said to Paro flatteringly.

Paro came even closer to him, held his hand and placed it back of her waist, held Krishna close to her body and landed a kiss on his cheek. Krishna was on cloud nine with the unexpected first kiss from her. Krishna put his arms around her neck and said, "You are in a good mood today. You are out for a kill! Uh?"

"You have forgotten today is my birthday."

"Happy birthday Paro."

She drew back. "Where is my gift?"

"Gift, oh yeah!" Krishna pulled her closer to his body and kissed her. "Here is your gift, my love."

"One more, you are such a passionate kisser, I hardly knew."

Krishna obliged.

Someone had entered through the front door. Footsteps heard in the drawing room, a minute later Dipti came in. "You both having fun, eh?" She turned to her handbag and picked a neatly packed gift and handed over to Paro. "Happy Birthday, Paro."

Krishna had brought a gift for her. He pulled out a 5-Star bar from his pocket and said, "Many happy returns of the day."

"I thought you did not remember today is my birthday."

"How can I not remember?" replied Krishna.

Paro kept aside the gift, and they shared the 5-Star bar among themselves getting ready for the tutorials. Dipti reminded them, Professor Majumdar will show the answer scripts. Krishna became tensed. He had not done well in the test. By this time Bhabhiji and Nimmi had returned. They shifted to the drawing room. Krishna was rather tense and waited for Professor Majumdar.

Professor Majumdar came with the answer scripts and showed it to them. Dipti had scored 62%; Paro scored 77%, and Krishna had obtained 64%.

"Not up to my expectation, all silly mistakes," commented Professor Majumdar.

Krishna replied back, "Had I come prepared; I would have scored much higher, but 64% upsets me."

"When will you wake up?" Professor Majumdar was furious with Krishna.

"You should have completed the task that I had given in the last class. Time is running out. Pay attention to your studies and prepare well for your board exam. You have very little time." Krishna sat in the chair with this head down in shame.

Bhabhiji brought in plates of Bengali sweets and informed Professor Majumdar that it was Paro's birthday today. Professor Majumdar began the tutorial class. Krishna was not paying attention to the class. He was daydreaming. Krishna sat in the chair and constantly stared at Paro. Paro stared back at Krishna as she ate the sweets from her plate. Dipti watched them very closely and could not control herself and touched Krishna on his wrist to remind him that they were in a classroom setting. Professor Majumdar noticed this.

"Today, you people are in no mood to study. It is Parmeet's birthday, so I am letting you go."

He excused them for the day. Krishna was very pleased. He realized that he could be with Paro the whole evening. Paro was jubilant. She quickly got up and said, "I will get the camera. We will take some pictures."

They went out in the garden. Paro called Nimmi who took many pictures in and around the garden. They spent the rest of the day chit-chatting until late in the evening. Paro's elder brother returned home only then Krishna parted from her for the long journey home.

ACID TEST

The fun-filled days of college were now over. Krishna had appeared for the board examination thus completing his two years in college. He appeared for medical entrance examination as well. The pressure of examinations fatigued him. Moreover, he was feeling homesick. He wanted to meet with his parents and siblings. Soon after the board examination, Paro left for Punjab to visit her parents. The summer vacation at school was to begin soon. His father had written a letter to him that they were coming down. He waited patiently at Hooghly for them to arrive. Within a week's time of his siblings' school closing for vacation, his family was in Hooghly visiting him. His parents had planned a trip this vacation. He went with his family to the hills visiting Darjeeling and its neighborhood places. It was a long awaited holiday. They had been to a family trip last about three years ago as he was also away from his family for the last two years. Krishna enjoyed the trip very much.

After a 15-day trip, he was back to his hometown of Hooghly. His family stayed with him for a few days before they returned to Belpahar. By then, it was time for the results to be out and tension started to build up again.

At first, the medical entrance exam results came in. He could not secure a seat. How could he? Those who lock themselves up in a room in the pile of books for these two years can probably make it. But Krishna was having a pretty good time with friends during this period. He was merrymaking his new found liberty that his father gave him. He lacked the direction and the mindset to make it possible. Did he want to be a doctor? I don't think so. He surely would have worked hard for it. He wanted to become a doctor only because many family members were doctors. His parents had not pressurized him either, but he could not face them.

This was just the beginning; a shocking news came in. Lockout declared at the Dunlop factory. He worried about Paro and her family. Paro was away at her parental home and had not yet returned. He visited Paro's residence and met with Bhabhiji. She was worried as she was not sure where they were heading. She shared with Krishna that the Dunlop factory might not open in near future as the management was not eager to keep it running. Over and above all this, Paro was away at her parental home somewhere in Punjab. He could not think how this situation would turn out to be. His days were passing in anxiety.

One of these days, the board examination result was declared. Krishna went to the college to know about his result. The results were on the notice board. He went through the list looking for his roll number and name. He found that he had secured 56%. Then he looked for Paro's score. She had scored 68% and Dipti 67%. James, Joy, Manoj had obtained scores in the 50s and 60s; Sandeep and Ravi had done better, scoring in 70s and 80s.

Krishna was shocked to see such a poor performance by him. He was depressed and sulking. He came home quietly and shut himself up. This happens when one loses track of what one wants to achieve. No substitute for hard work. A substantial amount of dedication and hard work goes in during these two years. They have not been easy for anyone so far and would not have been for him either. The damage was already done. Shame and guilt engulfed him as he felt he had let his parents down. His father called him up and said, "Son, don't worry, get yourself a graduation degree. You should work hard and not let me down." At the end of the call with his father, he felt relieved. His problems were far from over. The college had fewer seats for the degree program, and he had to secure a place for himself.

The following day, Dipti was at his doorstep. She said, "Paro has come back. She wants to meet you." That very evening he went to meet Paro. Paro looked sad and pensive. He could not understand why she felt that way. She had done well and secured good marks as expected.

He asked, "You should be happy with your results. Why are you so sad?"

Paro broke the news. "I have to go from here. My parents have asked me to complete my education in Punjab. They don't want to put undue pressure on my brother anymore."

Furthermore, in the conversation with Paro, he could come to know that her elder brother was offered voluntary retirement and probably he will take it.

This news gave him the biggest shock of his life. It left him with a heavy heart. He experienced as if the whole sky fell on his head. He was still as a stone. He could realize that the world that he had painstakingly built had gone further away from him and beyond his means to hold it together. He did not know what to do. He assessed the situation before him. He has failed to obtain a seat in medical, and then a miserable result in board exam. Over and above this, Paro was leaving. Will he ever be able to see her again?

He asked, "Will I be able to see you again?"

"I don't know," she replied.

"Krishna, what will you do next?"

"First, I have to obtain a seat in the college for graduation. I want to study computers."

"A wise choice indeed! Have you checked with any institute?"

"No, not yet. I was waiting for the results."

"Results are out; you should check it out."

"How long will you be here?"

"I am leaving tomorrow." Krishna was shocked yet again.

"Couldn't you stay a few more days?"

"I have to join college. The results were out when I left. The forms will be available from this week."

"Oh, God! you are telling me now. Just another 24 hours!"

"This is my address, keep writing. I expect a mail every week from you."

"What about the phone?"

"We live in a village. We do not have the phone in our house."

"When is the train?"

"Tomorrow at 6:15 p.m."

"So, you will be leaving in the evening, and this is our last evening together."

"Krishna, I love you. It is very difficult for me to be without you, but I have no other choices."

"What choices do I have?"

"If God permits, we may meet again."

"You are leaving tomorrow. I will come and meet you tomorrow."

"No, Krishna, please! Please don't come tomorrow. I can't cry anymore. I have been crying for days since my father told me. It will be very difficult for me to control myself tomorrow."

Paro sobbed slowly and looked at Krishna.

"Krishna, you are crying?" A drop of tear had rolled down his cheek.

"Yes, I am. My whole world has fallen apart. I can't think of anything."

They sat silently together for the last time holding each other's hand and watching the sun set over the western horizon.

LIFE'S PLAYS RUN FAST

Krishna is back to where he had started. The only difference now was, two years had passed. He is again getting ready for a seat in college as previously. Hopefully, he has learned from his mistakes. The two years that had passed will never come back. What could he do now? The opportunity of making something big in life had gone forever. Moreover, he had also lost his sweetheart, Paro, the only source of inspiration that had helped him through these two years. She was not around, and this made him feel it was not worthwhile to go to the same college. He knew that whenever he would be here, he would remember her, and it would be very tormenting for him to face his friends who would constantly ask him about her.

Within a few days, he came to know that Sandeep secured a place in engineering and had left for the same. Then came the news of Joy, he too was moving to another college for the subject he wanted to pursue was not available in the college. Manoj's father paid a handsome amount to reserve a seat in engineering for him somewhere in Bangalore. Why these Bangalore colleges sell seats made Krishna wonder. Could he have asked his father for the same? No, he never asked for it. He knew his father would have to take a loan to meet his aspiration. It would be a debt for the family, and he never wanted this to happen. He has already messed up once. He could not afford to do it again. He believed he had something else to do than buy out a seat for himself.

He knew he was in one of the metro cities of the country, a great opportunity for him. A lot happens here. He should venture out for something new, the one that no one had tried before. He wanted to learn computers. Many years ago, he had seen a computer in his father's office for the first time. These were the days when the PC revolution had not yet begun. The computer was not what we see nowadays. A large box which looked like a filing cabinet in any office. It fascinated him. He always wanted to learn more about it. Since then a few years had passed. Therefore, he wanted to pursue a career in computers. Very few students had ventured into this domain. The technology was very primitive, and the PC revolution had just come into India and was beyond the reach of common man.

After Paro's departure, he was very lonesome and sad, but could he do anything to hold her back. Could he? He often wondered how he could stop Paro from going back to Punjab. He often fondly remembered her, and this led him to depression. Furthermore, some of his best friends had moved on. He had little interest to go to the same college and continue his education.

One day, a sudden realization struck him, thinking aloud "what is this happening to me. I am losing control over my life. Come on, get over it. You got to carry on with your life. You had always taken substantial risks in your life," reminding himself of the day when he for the first time left home, the security of his parents, and joined the college in standard 11, took a leap into the unknown all alone.

"What have I got to do next? Should I leave the college as Paro will not be here anymore or try somewhere else?" Such intrinsic thoughts were troubling him. "Okay, first things first! Check out the computer institute," he told himself.

Computer institutes nowadays are in every small town and village of the country. But then, such education was available in the metros only. Krishna knew of only a handful of institutes in Kolkata. Thus he did not have too many options available to him. He wanted to do this course part-time along with his graduation. He went through the newspaper advertisements, and he found only one institute offered courses recognized by the Government of India. He immediately called up the institute to inquire about it.

He asked the lady on the phone, probably a receptionist, "I am interested in learning computers. When are the classes held?"

"It is mostly at weekends, are you a graduate?"

"No, I am not, but will be soon. Do you have anything to offer?" inquired Krishna.

"Come to our office today; I will let you know the details."

"I won't be able to make it today. I will visit tomorrow."

"Meet you tomorrow."

"Thank you so much." Krishna disconnected the line.

The following day he was off to the institute. The institute was in the heart of Kolkata on the 12th floor of the tallest building near Park Street. Park Street area is the most happening place of Kolkata. Major offices housed in the tall buildings. A few shopping complexes and food joints have sprung up lately. Movie theaters all around.

Those days, students from science background were allowed to pursue computer education, that too preferably pure science graduates. Krishna met with the receptionist with whom he had spoken over the phone. She sent him to meet with Preeti, the counselor. It was tough for Krishna to convince Preeti to allow him to join the course as it was a postgraduate course and one had to be a graduate to apply.

Krishna showed his certificates that he had brought along to Preeti. Preeti's attention went to his certificates from school. She said, "Hey! You are from Belpahar. Do you remember me?"

Krishna was rather surprised. He could not think of anyone called Preeti at Belpahar. She was at least five years elder to him. He tried to rake his memory, but still could not figure it out who she was. She said, "Can you recollect Mr. S. K. Chatterjee. He worked under your father?"

"Oh, yes! It must be over seven years now since he left Belpahar. Now, I remember! We frequently visited your house."

"Yeah! It was a small community; everyone knew everyone. Isn't it? How is life at Belpahar?" she asked.

"Belpahar has grown over the years, but it has lost its old charm," remarked Krishna.

"Okay Krishna, since I know you, I will let you do the postgraduate course, but you will not get the certificate unless you produce your graduation certificate."

"That is fine with me. Thank you very much" replied Krishna.

The computer classes at the institute were to begin the following month. Krishna had to secure a place for himself in graduation. He always had to think hard about the alternatives and decide for himself. He could blame none for a wrong decision. He did listen to advice from elders in the family, but at the end, it was his decision. He always did whatever he thought to be best at that time. So far, it seemed to work out well for him. He never regretted his decision; otherwise, he would not have been here. He would have remained in Belpahar forever.

Subsequently, he had to enroll in a degree course. He thought, let me go to the college and check when the forms will be made available. With this in mind, he went to the college. The good old days reminded him of the events as he went past various departments in the Science Block. He went to each department and met his professors. They insisted that he obtain a seat here as no other colleges nearby offered the quality education that they had to offer.
"Why take chances? I will graduate from here."

He collected the application forms and filled it up there and deposited at the office. He wanted to know about the number of seats available. He came to know that 20 seats were there in Biosciences stream in the college. He spoke with his principal about his interest to study Biosciences. The principal told him that he would make some arrangement for him as he had been a prominent member of the college union. He did have a chance. Krishna's worries were gone for now. He went to the administrative officer of the college. "Sir, I want a seat in Biosciences stream. I have deposited the form. Please take care."

"Don't worry, Krishna. We would always ensure that our boys remain with us."

"Thank you, I hope my grade is not a hindrance."

"We will do something about it for you. Meet me tomorrow at 3 p.m., after the selection committee meeting is over."

Krishna had to wait for another day. The following day, he visited the administrative officer at his office. He said, "The list is on the notice board, go check it out."

He went to the notice board and found his name listed among the 20 students who opted for Biosciences. He was happy and content in what he had achieved. He was overjoyed to see James and Pinky were in his class.

Krishna had not met James for a long time. It is the time that he visits him now. He went to James's house to meet with him. It was a hot sunny afternoon and James was fast asleep in his bed. He went and woke him up.

"You, lazy bones! Get up. How can you sleep tight in the afternoon?" James woke up rubbing his eyes. He said that he had been to the college, but came back home exhausted, so he slept.

"Do you know, the list is out. We are together again."

"Yes, I know. I am coming from the college," replied Krishna.

James's mom brought in some tea for them. James always has his tea at his bedside whenever he woke up, be it morning or afternoon. After having his tea, James said, "Let us go out."
"Where will you go in this hot summer afternoon?"
"It 3 o'clock now. It is pretty hot outside." James pushed the thick window curtain and looked at the sky.
"Let us go to the riverside. It will be a pleasant place to be in the afternoon."

They both were off to the riverside. Benches were put along the riverside facing the river and large trees along the banks gave ample shade around them. A great relief for the people who were out in the sun in the afternoon. People often used to sit on the benches under the trees or even sleep under it to beat the heat as a cool breeze blew. But today, as they occupied one of those benches, no breeze blowing from the river Ganges. Everything looked so still and quiet. The river Ganges was now at low tide, no boats in the river.

James asked, "What is the news of Parmeet?"

Krishna wanted to avoid answering, but James would not let him go, he had to reply.
"She has gone back to her parents in Punjab."
"How could she leave you like this?" asked James.
"You are aware of the Dunlop situation, don't you?"
"Oh, yeah! But..."

Krishna quickly interrupted him and said, "Her father asked her to come back."
"You are missing her a lot, isn't it? I feel like I lost a good friend," remarked James.

"I initially thought so, and I did not want to go to the college, but for the past two days, as I was in the college, I could feel her presence around me. It reminded me of those good old days and felt so refreshed. Even though she is not here anymore, I don't know why I was feeling so calm and composed and my mind filled with joy. Maybe I was happy about the seat in the degree course. I am still not very sure why?"

"You were in the state of trance," remarked James.

"What?"

"Whenever one attains this state, happiness flows like a river. This is in Bhagavad-gita," mentioned James.

"Don't tell me! You are a Christian. How do you know all this?"

"I spent a few months with some sages who had come down from the Himalayas. They taught me a few things."

What was it?

"Look at those leaves in the trees."

Krishna looked at the tree. As there was no breeze blowing and the air was still, the leaves were not moving at all.

"I do not see anything other than leaves in that tree," remarked Krishna.

"Keep looking for five minutes."

Krishna kept looking at it. A minute or two passed, he noticed one or two leaves started moving. Then, slowly cool breeze started to blow from the river towards him. It relaxed their senses. Krishna kept wondering what is happening. He was very surprised. From nowhere, the breeze was blowing over a limited area.

"You can control nature!"

"No, no one can control nature. Everything is there. It exists in the universe in its own time and space. What only that one needs to do is to ask for it. It will come to you," replied James.

Krishna was surprised to hear this from James. He had not seen this part of James before. He appeared to be in the state of higher consciousness.

"Hinduism is a perfect path to God, but people have reduced it to a mere mockery and have therefore lost its identity," said James.

Krishna still could not figure out was this a mere coincidence or something else. But whatever James had said even though he was a Christian was very true. We don't understand ourselves very well. A whole new world beyond what we can perceive through our senses. We always tend to believe what we see, and that turns out to be an illusion. We are also not accepting of what are yet to see, as we believe, "seeing is believing" and most of us will agree. The common sense alone cannot understand the Absolute Truth. James was no magician, just an ordinary boy like Krishna, but probably his association with learned sages led him to a higher understanding.

Who is calling?

Krishna had his share of anxiety, distress, and depression thus far. He had faced the waves of misery that came onto him. Somehow he had managed to overcome it. Now, that he had secured a seat for his graduation in his college and was pursuing a career in computer education, he was better placed to face the challenges of life. He had a vision in life that he put forth for himself.

He was very relaxed by now. The college reopens next month and along with it his computer classes. He had to go to the institute thrice a week, Wednesday, Saturday, and Sunday for computer classes. He had a hectic schedule on Wednesday. After his college which ended by noon, he had to rush to Kolkata to the computer institute. He was not required to go to college on Saturday and Sunday as they were his off days. He was now relaxed and spending his time leisurely watching television.

One afternoon, he was watching the cricket match on the television in his drawing room along with his cousin brother, two years younger. The telephone rang. As his cousin did not leave the couch to receive the phone, he walked toward the small desk at the far end of the room and picked up the phone.

"This is Mitra's residence, who is calling please?"

"Yeah! I know that. You need not tell me," a female voice he could not recognize as he had not heard it before.

"Whom do you want to speak to?"

"Mr. Mitra," replied the girl.

"Uncle is not at home."

"No, not your uncle, Mr. Mitra please," mentioned the girl.

"So, you want Abhay, right!" He called out, "Abhay, your phone."

"No, no, not him. Give the phone to junior Mitra."

"Nobody else lives here, a wrong number."

"No, the number is right, don't joke! Please, give the phone to junior Mitra," persuaded the girl.

"Nobody else around, I told you before."

"How stupid of you. Can't you call junior Mitra? Do you live here? Are you a member of the family? Who are you?" The girl giggled. This was not funny. Krishna was annoyed. "You whore! Don't you have anything else to do?"

He banged the receiver disconnecting the line.

"Who called? Why were you abusive? Where is your telephone etiquette by the way?" said Abhay still seated on the couch watching the match.

"Some stupid girl played a prank."

"What did she say?"

"I presume the call was meant for you."

"I do not receive calls from girls. Father is very strict with the phone. I study in boy's school. I don't have a girlfriend."

"You might have given the number to someone you know."

"She should have asked for me."

"Oh, yeah!, when I mentioned your name, she did not want to talk to you."

They brainstormed about the caller, but could not identify anyone they knew of among their friends or family friends. Her voice did not sound similar to anyone he knew. Krishna could not recollect if he gave his telephone number to anyone else. He knew none of his friends would dare to play a prank on him, and he would easily identify them. The caller appeared childish to him. They were unable to identify the caller.

"We will wait for another 10 minutes, she may call again," remarked Krishna. There was no further call. Finally, Krishna said, "That was a perfect treatment for her. She will never try again. Let's go and watch the match."

No further calls came that day. The day passed uneventfully, and Krishna had forgotten about the incident. In those days, there were many incidences of cross-connections happening quite often, but nothing like this.

The following day, at 4:15 p.m., the phone rang again. Krishna was just about to leave his home for a game of cricket with his friends. He rushed to the phone and picked it up. "Mitra's residence, who is calling please?" The same girl had called again.

"There you are. I demand an apology."

"Apology? for what?"

"You were calling names yesterday. Come on, be quick. You owe me an apology."

"Apology! My foot! I owe no apology."

"You don't know how to speak to a lady either." She taunted Krishna yet again and laughed at him. Krishna realized he should not have spoken those words yesterday.

"Okay, I apologize, I am sorry."

"That's better. Your name?"

"I won't tell you."

"What is wrong with you? Do you behave in this way with everyone?"

"No, I do not speak to strangers."

"But, we met yesterday."

"When?"

"We spoke yesterday, you fool!" laughing aloud.

"What is your name?" she asked again.

"I have not seen you before. You are a guest?"

"Err…I am…Sudhir."

"So you are Sudhir. Since how long have you been visiting here?"

"I am not a visitor. I live here. This is my house."

"Never heard of you before."

"You know my name. Tell me yours."

"Hold on, meet my sister." She handed over the phone.

"Hi! there."

"What do you want from me?"

"Nothing."

"Why are you calling?"

"Just like that."

"What is your name?"

"We don't have any. Why don't you give one."

"Give the phone back to me." Krishna overheard a conversation at the other end. The girls were eager to talk to him. The caller was back. "This is fun," Krishna said to himself.

"Do I know you?"

"Maybe."

"I do not remember meeting you. Are you in school or a college?" She did not reply to the question, instead asked, "What about my name?"

"Well…..er..I do not know you. Therefore I would call you Anamika."

"That's a nice name. What about my sister's."

"I have to give her a name too."

"Yes, do you have one?"

"Since she is your sister, perhaps Anjana."

"That is pretty good," she replied. Someone is coming, she told her sister.

"We have to go. Bye!"

"May I have your number please?"

"Sorry, next time, bye."

The line was disconnected. Krishna did not know what to do next. He thought he should talk it out with James. James could throw some light on this episode. Krishna met with James the following day and shared the entire episode.

"Krishna, I will find out who they were."

"When?"

"Not now."

"Today?"

"Not today, we will meet tomorrow at your home."

The following day, James came to Krishna's house. He informed Krishna that Pinky had his telephone number, but ruled out Pinky could be the one. He suggested that the caller must be known to Pinky. The caller got hold of his number and knew him through Pinky, who played the mischief. Krishna did not agree with James as the girl had a childish tone. James suggested that they talk to Pinky. Krishna agreed, and they called Pinky and told her about the entire episode.

Pinky patiently heard him and finally said, "Yesterday, as I walked into my room, I saw my cousins talking to someone on the phone. They hurriedly disconnected."

"I told you, we nailed them," said James.

"Your cousins? How do they know me?"

"Just the other day, we talked about college, and I told them about you. I can't imagine they would make a call to you."

Trio Again

A week later, Krishna was on his way to the computer institute. He bought a new notebook and left for Kolkata. As he entered the institute on the 12th floor, there were a large number of students waiting to enter the classroom. There was only one classroom, and class was going on. He waited along with others. After a while, the class was over, and a large number of students came out of the classroom. He then rushed to occupy a chair in the front row. There weren't any. He moved to the second row and took a seat. The boy who sat next him was of his age, very smart and handsome. The boy turned towards Krishna and said, "I am Parthasarathi, final year student from Asutosh College." "Krishna, from Hooghly Mohsin College." "Let us be friends." "Of course."

A knock heard at the door. A girl was standing at the door of the classroom. She had a large leather brown handbag in her arm. Her hair was short, just little below her shoulders. She wore a light green colored tee with a picture of "Tweety" on it.

"May I come in sir."

She came in and was looking for a seat. The seat next to Parthasarathi was still vacant.

She said, "May I sit here please."
"Okay" replied Parthasarathi.
"I am Riya Sen, and you?"
"I am Partha.... Parthasarathi and meet Krishna," introducing Krishna to Riya.
"Hi, Krishna!"
"Hi, Riya!"

The faculty walked into the classroom. All the students stood up and greeted him.

He introduced himself. "I am Dr. Srinivas; I will be covering two modules, one in this semester and one in the next."

Dr. Srinivas introduced the importance of computers to the class and started the class right away.

Krishna was spell-bound with the introductory class by Dr. Srinivas. He explained every little detail to the class. At the end of the class, Dr. Srinivas mentioned to students that they had to form a team of three members for the hands-on session and enlist themselves with the administrative staff. As they left the classroom, Partha said, "Let's get together." Riya noticed she had to find two members to team up with said, "Take me in."
"Okay, Riya, you are in," replied Krishna. Krishna was ready with his team.

They walked into the front office area and sat on the sofa.

"Do you have a girlfriend?" Riya asked Krishna.

"Why do you ask?"

"Tell me, please."

"Yes, I do, but she is now far away."

"Where is she?"

"Punjab."

"That is very far off. What is her name?"

"Parmeet."

"How long have you been seeing her?"

"Two years."

"What about you Partha?" asked Riya turning to Partha.

"Childhood sweetheart from my good old school days," replied Partha with a big smile on his face.

"Where is she? Can I meet her?" inquired Riya rather inquisitively.

"She is in Raniganj. I did my schooling there. My parents are also there."

Krishna could realize that Partha also had a similar upbringing like him. He too was away from his parents. Krishna could feel his emotions very well. He could see that they both were in the same situation and therefore bonded very well.

"I too have a boyfriend. I know him for the past six months."

"Before that?" questioned Partha.

"I did have a childhood crush on a boy, the football captain of the school team."

"And then?" remarked Krishna.

"That ended there. I did date for 7 to 8 months with one of my college buddies before I met Srikanth."

She went on to say that Srikanth is a model and a struggling actor. He has done some assignments and is having talks with some director for a role in a Bengali movie. She also mentioned that her boyfriend is very possessive. He does not allow her to meet with or talk to anybody. He is always following her wherever she went. That was the reason why she was late to the class. She had to evade him and come to this class.

Krishna, Partha, and Riya met with Preeti to schedule their computer lab. Preeti informed that Dr. Srinivas was a visiting faculty from Jadavpur University. He has many books to his credit. They should make the best use of this opportunity to learn from such a renowned scholar and author. Meanwhile, Riya went to the manager's cabin and was busy talking to him. Partha and Krishna waited for a while and left the institute. They went down to the ground floor lobby and waited for Riya to come. After about 10 minutes, Riya came down the lift, but went past Partha and Krishna and stood at the bus stop. Krishna and Partha followed Riya to the bus stop. Krishna did not realize why Riya was annoyed with him.

"What happened Riya?"

"Everyone is the same."

"We came down and were waiting for you here in the ground floor lobby."

"I went to talk with the manager for a minute, and I could not find you. I searched you everywhere in the institute. Then somebody said you had already left." She held a small handkerchief tightly in her hand with which she wiped her tears to stop it roll down her cheek.

"I am sorry Riya, I will never leave you again," said Krishna. They waited for Riya to board a bus on her way home.

"Riya is so soft. She was all over you." Partha put his right arm around Krishna and walked with him along the footpath.

"You must be joking," replied Krishna.

Partha smiled and said, "Marry Riya and she will become Riya Mitra."

"She already has a boyfriend, and she is elder to me."

"One to two years this way that way does not matter," replied Partha.

"Wow! What an idea *Sirjee*, Brooke Shields marries James Bond and she becomes Brooke Bond!"

"I admire your sense of humor!"

Krishna was very deeply in love with Paro. He always felt she was very much a part of his life. He used to write letters to her regularly.

Over the weekend, this trio met again for a computer hands-on. Krishna was late for the class. He found Riya and Partha waiting outside the computer lab.

Partha said, "You are late."

"I am sorry. I was stuck in the traffic."

"Let's go," said Riya.

They were in the computer lab for practical hands-on. It was their first assignment. The computers in those days had two 5-1/2 inch floppy drives, drive A and B. MS-DOS 3.2 was the operating system. One had to insert the floppy in drive A to boot the system. The CPU had an Intel processor 8088 series and had a large cabinet. The RAM was only of 640 KB. The monitor placed over the CPU cabinet. The display was a cathode ray tube like that of old television sets and two knobs to adjust the brightness and contrast. The display was either fluorescent green or fluorescent orange monochrome display. The computer systems were then called PC – personal computer, a PC-XT – the extended technology had a built in hard drive. Finally, the best of the lot, the most advanced state-of-art was the PC-AT with an Intel processor 80286 often referred as AT-286.

The trio walked into the computer lab. Krishna saw a PC for the first time before him. Three chairs placed for students to sit and work on the computer. The computer was at the top of a desk. Krishna took the chair at the center and Partha and Riya on his either side. He looked at the keyboard. It resembled that of a typewriter but with a few more keys on it. Krishna kept wondering what the utility of so many keys. The lab assistant walked up to them and showed them how to switch on the computer and the booting process. He inserted a 5-1/2-inch floppy in the drive A to loaded the operating system into its memory. The system was ready for use; a prompt; drive A> and the cursor blinking.

"Let me try first." Krishna took out his notebook to copy the assignment and enter into the computer and test run it. Krishna had to look for each letter in the keyboard, find it and press it with the index finger. The first assignment was to create a file, save it on disk A, and then copy it to disk B. This was all he had to do, apart from learning a few other

DOS commands. The test run was successful on his first attempt.

"You are pretty quick! How do you do that?" acclaimed Partha.

"I had purchased a book on MS-DOS from the book fair."

"You should lend me the book."

"Okay, I will lend you for a day or two."

It was now the turn of Partha and Riya to do their assignments. Partha tried his hands on the computer. He was quick to adapt. He also completed his assignment with ease. They now instructed Riya with her assignment. Partha wanted to make the best use of the time they were together.

"We should do joint studies."

"Oh, yeah! it will be very helpful for us," replied Riya.

"Okay, that is a great idea," replied Krishna.

"Where do we study?" asked Riya.

"Here in the institute," replied Partha.

"Not here," said Riya.

"Okay, let us get out of the institute and then we will decide," said Krishna. They came down to the ground floor lobby.

"Where do we go?" questioned Riya.

"Victoria," said Partha.

"It will be crowded," remarked Krishna.

"We will find a place to sit," said Partha.

Victoria Memorial Hall is a very important landmark of Kolkata. Victoria Memorial is a large marble building and has a museum. This building is dedicated to the memory of Queen Victoria. It is one of the most visited tourist spots. Many visitors from far and near come here in the evenings.

Families come with children for the picnic, and to have fun and play on the sprawling lawns.

Victoria Memorial is situated at the center of the estate with many water bodies, lawns, gardens, trees all over the whole area. The lawns have sidewalks all the way around the water bodies. This is also a place where lovers met and spent their time together. They sit on the benches in pairs, sometimes more than one pair in a bench; many more pairs under the shade of huge trees all around the park.

It makes me wonder, why Partha chose this place. It was not an ideal place to study. Nevertheless, they all agreed and took a bus ride to Victoria. They entered through the North Gate of the Victoria Memorial. They leisurely walk around the large lawns of Victoria Memorial and noticed all benches occupied all around. Finally, they found a tree and sat under it. Krishna was prompt to take out the books from his bag. He began the discussion of the assignments given to them by Dr. Srinivas. They studied there under the tree without paying attention to anything and everything going all around them. The sun was setting. The birds were returning to their nest, many species of birds chirping in the trees all around them. Suddenly, a very fair and handsome man stood behind Riya.

"I need to talk to you, come right away," said the man.

"Who is this? Do you know him?" remarked Krishna.

Riya was still engrossed in her notebook and taking notes of the assignments from Krishna's notebook.

"Do you know her?" asked Partha.

"Ask her," replied the man.

Riya said, "Srikanth!"

Krishna could not believe his eyes. He was astonished to see Srikanth standing before them. He suddenly did what no one expected of him. He quickly laid himself on Riya's lap and looked eye to eye with Srikanth. Srikant did not utter a word. He walked away exasperatedly.

This is the story of how Krishna met Partha and Riya. There was immense bonding between them. Many of his classmates at the institute felt Riya was dating with two of the classmates simultaneously. This did not bother the trio. They were best friends. They used to visit local food joints and watch movies together. Sometimes, Riya used to accompany them, especially when they went watching movies on Sunday.

Here, Krishna's college reopened. He had enrolled in the degree program. He had to study very hard. This time, he toiled day and night to keep abreast with the curriculum at college as well as the computer institute. He used to study late through the night and then go in the early morning to the college. As soon as he finished his college; he would rush back home and leave for the institute. He would spend hardly spend 30 minutes at home, having his lunch, changing his dress, switching his books and materials from the bag in preparation to go to the institute especially on Wednesday.

In this way, two months had passed, one day Krishna was with James seated on the steps of the bathing ghat.

James said, "I want to learn computers. Is it very difficult?"

"No, not at all. I think it is easier than memorizing that we have been doing."

"That's great."

"This is programming. You need to write codes in computer language."

"Won't you teach me?"

"Of course, yes!"

"My mother wants to meet you."

James took Krishna to his house. Krishna met with James's mother who showed a keen interest in him studying computer. Krishna promised to help him out. He took James to the institute and introduced him to Preeti. After a counseling session with Preeti, James joined the institute, but he was in the subsequent batch.

ANTAKSHARI

Krishna had been over six months into his degree program. Krishna had chosen this course as he intended to complete his graduation at an earliest and simultaneously his computer course. He would have dual qualification then. He had taken a very bold step to make a better future for himself. He had very little time in hand. His father was retiring in a year's time. He had to make himself employable and find a suitable job so that he was not dependent on his dad. His father had been very supportive of him as he always said: "Do what you love and love what you do." He thought it would be easier for him to get a good job and it turned out to be true.

Krishna was back to his college. He liked his college very much. He did miss many of his old friends, but he had Pinky and James by his side. He still longed to see Paro, but she was not here for him. Paro was in her hometown in Punjab with her parents and brother's family. Paro wrote to Krishna regularly. Krishna used to bring those letters and read it to James. Sometimes, Pinky also used to be with him, and they used to remember Paro fondly. Without wasting time, Krishna used to reply to Paro's letters. He used to wait eagerly for the mail carrier to give him Paro's letter at his doorstep.

The classes at the college had started in full swing. The theory classes were for 50 minutes, and the practical classes were for 2 hours. Krishna was attending his college regularly. On the days he did not go to the computer institute, he used to prepare his notes of the lecture sessions in the college. He was now studying with James and Pinky, his old classmates and few others. His class had ten boys and ten girls. He never missed any lecture. The professors take a note of this and appreciate his efforts.

It is winter months. Students are excited. Winter holiday was just a week away. On one such day, he was seated with James and Pinky in the classroom.

"Let's go for a picnic," said Pinky.

"Picnic!" remarked James.

"Didn't you notice? Every day I see groups of people loaded into buses and trucks going to picnic with blaring loudspeakers as they go by. I want to go."

"Let the vacations begin," replied James.

"No, no, no! I want to go now. Please, please Krishna, do something."

"When you want to go, we go."

"Make it a class picnic."

"I will speak to them."

Krishna spoke to his classmates and convinced them to go for a picnic. He went to meet with Professor Majumdar and inform him of their plans for a picnic and seek his permission. They were to go to the picnic the subsequent Saturday. Krishna did not have any classes scheduled that week in his institute. Professor Majumdar gave the permission for a class picnic as they had already covered the syllabus for the semester.

Krishna arranged for a picnic spot in a nearby village by the river Ganges. That Saturday, all his friends gathered at college and then left for the picnic spot in a minibus. James had hired the bus; Krishna arranged for the food and groceries. Pinky arranged for the snacks and beverages, and two of their classmates volunteered to cook. The picnic spot was in an ashram compound. Krishna chose this place as he had come here before. It was fun-filled. They teamed up and did the cooking themselves and had a hearty meal. Krishna did take a few photographs at the picnic. The picnic helped Krishna to bond very well with all his classmates.

One day, the professor was yet to come into the classroom, students were waiting and 10 minutes had passed. Suddenly, a student said, "we are bored waiting here."

Pinky remarked, "it is boring, let us play Antakshari. Let us team up."

They formed two teams, ten members in each team. One of them began a song from a Hindi movie. A few other students joined in the chorus. The rule of the game is the subsequent team should begin with a subsequent song of their choice starting with the last syllable of the song sung previously. The team who can't find a song with the syllable loses and the other team wins. Each student had a huge library of the song, and this could go on for hours. As the game continued, two boys started to play the drums with their bare hands on the desk. The music enthralled Krishna.

Krishna went to the teacher's table and climbed onto it. He started to dance. Others started to clap with the rhythm of the drums. Five girls formed a ring around the desk holding hands and danced merrily.

Suddenly, the professor came in and stood at the door and watched them. Slowly, the clap died out, and drums stop beating. Krishna jumped off the table and ran off to the end of the classroom to escape punishment.

"What is this going on?" asked the professor.

Pinky stood up and said, "We were playing Antakshari sir."

"Krishna come here. Why were you on the teacher's table?"

"I am sorry sir."

"You should never stand on teacher's table, don't you know that?"

"Yes, sir, I am very sorry. I will never do it again."

Professor with a smile on his face remarked. "I liked your team work. It was enchanting! It reminds me of Brindavan."

Krishna escaped punishment. James, Pinky, and Krishna celebrated their great escape.

THREE YEARS LATER

Krishna was very busy with his schedule. He had to go to the college in the morning, and the evening he was at the institute for his computer class and hands-on sessions. His classes at the institute were going on very well. He kept himself ahead of class this time. He worked hard with his assignments and projects. Partha was his teammate for his projects. Partha's contribution to the project was worth mentioning. Months had passed. They were through with most of the modules covered in the course, but the final examination was two months away.

One of these days, a Saturday, Krishna was at the institute. Preeti called him to her cubicle.

"Krishna, come here, how is your preparation going on?"

"Good," replied Krishna.

"We have a live project. Are you interested?"

"Yes! Of course."

"Okay, go and meet with the manager."

Krishna went and met the manager immediately. The manager asked him if he was free tonight. He nodded his head.

"I need two students to work as a team."

"I will take Partha. He will join me."

"Fine, speak to him now and confirm me. The work has to finish tonight."

Krishna went and spoke with Partha who immediately agreed. They had to stay at the institute that night. Krishna called his home and informed that he would not able to come home that night. Partha went home only to come back late at night. Riya and Krishna were at the institute. Riya took this opportunity to spend the evening with Krishna.

"Where will you go now?" asked Riya.

"I do not know. I will hang around till Partha returns."

"Come let's get out of here."

"Where do you want to go?"

"Nandan," replied Riya.

Krishna and Riya took a cab to Nandan. Nandan is a government-sponsored film and cultural center the heart of the city. Cultural programs are held here from time to time where young, and vibrant Bengal is showcased. Artist from all parts of Bengal come here and participate in the cultural festival. During the winter months, this place is buzzing with activities. Many artists from various parts of the world converge here bringing along with them their music, musical instruments, and dance forms.

Today, Nandan had no such program. Krishna could not understand why Riya wanted to go to Nandan. Despite his doubts, he agreed to go to Nandan with Riya. Interestingly, Nandan has also been a meeting place for many who look for a quiet place far from the madding crowd in the heart of the city. They took the tube railway to reach Nandan just two stations apart. They sat on a bench under a tree.

"Why are we here?" asked Krishna.

"I want to spend this evening with you."

"We could have gone for a movie."

"No, I wanted to talk to you."

"What's up?"

"I broke up with Srikanth!"

"Really, what happened?"

"I was suffocating with him. He was a real control freak. He did not permit me to do things that I wanted. He was very envious of my friends and especially you."

"I suspected that. Nevertheless, he was not good for you."

"What about you Krishna? How is Parmeet?"

"She is good. She is busy with her studies."

"There you go! When did you last see her?"

"Day before she left for Punjab."

"That must be a long time ago."

"Yeah! Exactly one year two months seventeen days."

"You are still waiting for her. Will she come back?"

"I don't know."

"You don't know! You should know. Why are you spoiling your life for her?"

"I love her. We are in touch."

"Letters!"

"How many did you receive this month?"

"One!"

"I am telling you she must be going around with someone."

"No! Never!

"Aren't you aware Krishna, out of sight is out of mind."

"You are telling me this because you broke up with Srikanth!"

"Yes I broke up, but the reasons are pretty obvious. Just look at you, Krishna."

"What's the problem?"

"You have not met with your girlfriend for so long. I do not think you are going to make any headway. She is gone!"

"I have not lost hope. Someday we will be together again."

"Be practical Krishna! When will you grow up?"

I believe in God. He will show us the way."

"I believe in God too. I know if you carry on this way, this is not going to last."

"Well, time will tell."

"Now, I have to go home. Can you drop me home?"

"Okay, Riya I will drop you home and then go to the institute."

Krishna went along with Riya to her home in Tollygunge. Riya introduced to him to her family; her parents and especially her elder sister. Her elder sister, Ranjana, was very fond of him. Riya used to talk a lot about Partha and Krishna to her. Ranjana invited Krishna for dinner with them, and he gladly accepted. He then went back to institute for the night stay. Krishna had not rested the whole day. Partha returned to join Krishna at 9:30 at night. Partha brought a tiffin-box containing parathas and egg curry prepared by his mother. Krishna already had a hearty meal at Riya's house. He was not hungry at all, but he could not say that he already had his meal. He quietly shared the tiffin-box with Partha. They worked together the whole night and watched the streets of Kolkata, so quiet at night from the 12th-floor window of the institute. The silence of Kolkata was very intriguing for them.

The work given to them was payroll processing of a client. They had to do the data entry of the master database and also the attendance details of all employees for the month. They had to verify the entries and then run the payroll for the month program to generate the pay-slips for the month. It was a huge database and lot of entries and validations had to be done. At around 3 a.m., they could validate all the entries and run the payslip generation program. The payslip printing started and went on for two hours.

A bright red sun rose from the east. It is Sunday. They had a class scheduled at 9 a.m. Krishna and Partha had completed the task they were given to them last night. They had a sleepless night as they worked throughout. As the sun rose, the streets of Kolkata became busy with buses and cars plying on the streets. They came down to the street for breakfast. People were out in the streets for their morning walk. Shops were yet to open, and street food was only available for them. They walked over a mile looking for a good food joint. They found a local restaurant serving tea, bread toast with an omelet. They had breakfast at that restaurant. It was already 8:30. They rush to the institute.

Krishna and Partha came into the classroom and found students had already arrived for the class. Today, Krishna sat in the third row. He avoided sitting in the first as he was exhausted. Dr. Srinivas came in and started the class. As the class was going on Krishna felt sleepy. He could not keep himself awake for long. After a few nods, he fell asleep. Dr. Srinivas noticed Krishna dosing off.

"Hey Krishna, tell me what comes after this for-loop?"

"Another for-loop, sir," replied Krishna. He had woken up. He stood up rubbing his eyes.

"You were sleeping in my class?"

"Yes, sir."

"Well, your answer is correct. We need to continue with another for loop here to complete the process."

"Were you awake for last few minutes?"

"No sir, I slept off. I worked the whole night here in the institute. Your question woke me up."

Krishna and Partha met James at the corridor. Partha related the incident of Krishna falling asleep in the class to James. James was astonished to hear that Krishna was attentive even while sleeping in the class.

As days passed by, the examination fever catches on. Krishna had double trouble. The final examination of computer studies was in a month's time, and then his final exam of graduation. Everybody tensed at home. They were worried about his performance this time, but Krishna was looking way ahead of time to finish his degree and computer education and try to get a job to start earning. Krishna's father had retired after completing thirty years of service. He is happy to be back with his family.

THE LETTER

Krishna had been sick, down with fever for the last ten days. He had symptoms of a runny nose, sore throat, cough, hoarseness, and muscle aches. Along with these symptoms, he had a throbbing headache. He felt fatigued most of the time. He was unable to get out of bed and move around. A long absence of Krishna was worrisome for Partha. He called to know about his whereabouts. Realizing that he was down with fever, Partha decided to visit him. He also mentioned that he would inform Riya and bring her along. Partha met with Riya in the institute. Upon hearing the news of Krishna, Riya accepted to accompany him.

The following day, Partha and Riya came to Krishna's home. A doctor, a friend of Krishna's father, had come by for a visit to check on him. As soon as the doctor left, Partha and Riya came in.

"What did the doctor say?" asked Partha.

"Viral fever," replied Krishna.

"You have a fever for last ten days. This is not a good sign. You should get a blood test."

"Yes, the doctor also mentioned this today. I will get it tomorrow at the clinic."

"You will be better soon. I am waiting for you, Krishna," remarked Riya.

"Riya, I told you before."

"Keep quiet. Don't worry, Krishna."

"Yeah! I have a headache too."

"Take rest, Krishna. Get well soon."

Partha stood there and quietly listened but did not intervene. He knew very well that Riya had a soft corner for Krishna. He wanted Krishna to accept the reality of his relationship with Parmeet. He knew very well that this would not last long. He did not want to force upon Krishna to accept Riya straightaway. He believed that Krishna would eventually come to terms with the reality and accept Riya.

Krishna was in two minds. He did not want to leave Paro and go for Riya. He felt it would be unjust on his part to move on with Riya. He loved Paro so dearly that he could still feel her around him even though she was thousands of miles away and he had not seen her for a pretty long time. Whenever he closed his eyes, he was able to see Paro smiling, her eyes shining brightly. His love for her was so profound that he could not imagine life without her.

Paro had not written any letters to him for months now. He used to write at least one letter every fifteen days. He would eagerly wait for a reply but over the last few months, he had only received a postcard from Paro. He wanted to hear more from her, but in vain. He used to check with the mail carrier every day, but there was no letter from her. He was not sure what to make of it. He kept wondering; Paro has gotten so busy that she could not write an Inland letter to him. He was also worried that something terrible might have happened. He prayed to God for her safety.

After a few days, Krishna received a letter from Paro. He opened the envelope and started reading.

My Dearest Krishna,

It has been a long time since I have last heard from you. Since the day I came over here to my hometown, I have received just a few letters from you. What is wrong? Why don't you write to me? Please, please, please do write. I am eagerly waiting for your letters. It has been months since you last wrote to me telling about the computer course, but since then I have been waiting to hear from you. I think by now you must have completed the course and got a job too.

The time we spent together is the best period of my life. I came to know Indrani and Ravi are married. They sent me an invitation card. You must have attended their wedding. How was it? Indrani looks very beautiful in the photograph that she sent me.

What about the others? Are you still in touch with the rest. Many of our friends have moved on, but James and Pinky are still with you. It must be fun in their company. What about Anita? She did not reply to my letter, and I have not received yours either. Don't do this to me. Promise me; you will write to me as soon as you finish reading this letter.

As you are aware, I had to face many hardships after I came here. As this is the final year of college, I am preparing for the upcoming final exam. I have to do well, get good grades, and get a job. Just last month my father passed away. He had a massive stroke. I feel lonesome now. He was very close to me and loved me very much. My elder brother has a job in a sports goods manufacturer and exporter firm. Now, he maintains the family. He wishes to stop my studies and marry me off. I don't know what to do. I just want to finish my college for now and then perhaps take up a job as a teacher in the school in our village.

Please write in detail about yourself. What have you been doing? What are your plans? I am eagerly waiting to hear more from you. Now that you have finished reading take a pen and paper and write a reply.

With lots of Love,

Yours Paro.

Krishna was in a pensive mood. Why Paro's sufferings do not come to an end? She has been battling it out for so long. Why God took away her dad? The most loving people depart from your life just when you need them the most. This shouldn't have happened to Paro, at least not now. He opened the drawer of his study table and put the letter in the stack of letters that he had received from Paro.

Krishna never replied to this letter. He was confused. This was an awkward situation for him. He did not know what to do. Could he stop Paro's brother marrying her off? He knew very well her brother. If he had decided on something, he would not delay to put it into action. He never listened to Bhabhiji. Thus he had no chance. Could he go to Punjab and ask for her hand? What would he say? How would he present himself?. What would he tell his parents? How would his parents react? He would be a laughing stock in front of his family as well as Paro's.

THE DIALOGUE

A year at the computer institute was coming to an end. Most of the modules were complete, and Krishna had done well so far. The final exam was a few weeks away. On a Sunday, the last practical hands-on session, Partha was very disturbed. He could not concentrate well on the task and sat quietly and watched Krishna and Riya continue with the session. This behavior was worrisome for Krishna. He could not understand what was disturbing to Partha so much. He had done pretty well in all the modules and was sure to pass the exam with flying colors. He did not expect to see his dear friend in such a pensive mood.

"What's the matter?"

"I will tell you after the class."

"That's fine. We will sit in the ground floor lobby."

"Nothing has happened to him. His mood is off today," said Riya.

"No, Riya! I have never seen Partha like this before."

"Oh! He is just playing a prank. He often does."

"I will come to know. We are going to stay back after this class."

"I am sorry Partha; I can't stay. I have to reach home early today."

"That is fine. You can go home. Krishna will be here."

After the practical hands-on, the trio came down to the ground floor lobby and out to the bus stand. They waited for the bus to arrive. When the bus came, Riya boarded the bus bidding them goodbye. Partha and Krishna came back to the ground floor lobby and sat on the sofa.

"Now, tell me what is going through your mind right now."

"I have to sit for medical entrance!"

"That is fantastic! You will become a doctor!"

"I do not want to attempt the entrance test."

"But…. why?"

"I do not want to be a doctor anymore."

"So you wanted to be a doctor, eh!"

Partha mentioned to Krishna that his parents want him to become a doctor. He also had similar plans for himself some years ago, but later chose to study computers.

"Partha, I see a doctor in you. You should sit for the entrance exam."

"My preparations are not complete. I do not have time."

"The entrance exam is still two months away. You have done it before; you can do it now. This is your last chance."

"No, you do not understand, I have a situation here. My father will retire."

Partha went on to explain that his father was retiring soon and would be back to Kolkata. He was the only son in the family and had to do something very quickly.

"I have a family to take care, you know." He had a sister growing up pretty fast. He also had to think about her marriage.

"That is at least four years away for now and that your parents can take care."

Partha was very unclear what he wanted in life. On one hand, he had the dream of becoming a doctor, and on the other hand, he wanted to sacrifice his dreams and pursue computers to get a job as early as possible.

"Medical is a 7-year effort; just an MBBS degree is not sufficient. I would have to pursue MD as well. God knows how long this will take."

Krishna listened to Partha patiently, and then he said, "I think you should sit for the entrance. Start your preparations right away."

"What if I get through the entrance?"

"You should pursue medicine."

"Why?"

"I found that you have a very high flair for medicine. This is what you love."

"I will complete my computers and then I will look for a job."

"No, do not do that."

Okay, what about my father's retirement."

When is your father retiring?"

"In two years' time."

"Partha, you have unnecessarily stressed yourself."

"What makes you think so?"

"You have two years at least to go before your father's retirement. He will at least support you for these two years. Your sister's marriage is still a long way to go. She has four or more years to get married, perhaps six or seven. You should not worry. You have everything going right for you. I know you will make it."

"It costs a lot of money."

"You will be going to a government college. The cost is less compared to private institutions. I know pretty well your father will be able to pay for the tuition fees."

"What about my computer degree? What do I do with that?"

"As you are very much aware that now computer applications are in the medical field too. I am sure you will have many avenues in this field also as you are already well-versed with programming, and you also will be able to develop software."

Partha after hearing all this from Krishna, could not stop himself from asking Krishna.

"You have taken the same path, but why are you advising me?"

"Well, my situation is not equivalent to yours. My father retired three months ago."

"So what?"

"I am doing what I always wanted to do."

"So am I."

"No Partha, you are not. As I told you before, I have seen your keen interest in medicine. This is what you love. Go Partha! Go for it!"

"You are going the same path as I planned to do." Partha reiterated.

"No, Partha! It is not the same."

"I loved quite a few things as a child. I loved to draw and paint. It could be a hobby, but not a profession as told at school. I was told to choose between an engineer, doctor, or lawyer. My father is an engineer."

"So what did you choose?"

"I had to choose to be a doctor. It is a family tradition."

"Then what happened?"

"I saw a computer in my father's office. I loved it, something magical, I was fascinated by it."

"Oh, at that time you decided to be a computer programmer."

"Yes, I had been keeping it close to my heart for all these years. I came to know that I had to be a graduate to get enrolled two years ago. I could not wait for it, so I had asked Preeti if I could join earlier, and here I am."

"Good for us, they are allowing undergraduates to study part-time."

"Thank God! Otherwise, I had to wait another three years."

"Isn't it fantastic! Otherwise, we would not have met."

"My father always said, do what you love, love what you do! I tell you the same."

"Yes, I understood what he meant."

Krishna finally took a word from Partha that he would sit for the medical entrance.

The days seemed to fly off quickly. The final exam at the institute was over. Krishna was very confident. He had studied well. He was very satisfied with the papers. When the results came, he found that he and Partha had secured an A-plus grade, and Riya had also done well with an A grade. She was very happy that their friendship and studying together brought out the best of her.

Then the news of Partha's medical entrance results came. Partha also made to the ranking position that he could join the prestigious NRS Medical College. Partha went on to pursue his medical degree.

The graduation examination was to begin within a month of his computer exams. He prepared himself well for the examination as it was very important for him. He sat for graduation examination with full confidence. After a period of 2-3 months when the results came he had passed his graduation with flying colors. After receiving the mark sheet, he went to the computer institute to receive diploma certification.

At the institute, he met with Preeti and asked for his diploma certificate. She asked him to furnish his graduation marks sheet and to meet the manager. Krishna wondered why he was required to meet him. He shared his mark sheet to Preeti who requested him to give a photocopy instead. Krishna quickly took out a photocopy from his bag and handed over to Preeti. Krishna then waited in the waiting area to be called in by the manager.

After waiting for fifteen minutes, he was asked to meet with the manager. The manager told him that a reputed company was looking to hire executives, and he is being sent to meet with the personnel manager of the company today. The manager also mentioned that the office was two blocks away and handed him the card of the personnel manager. On his way out of the office, he met with Preeti who handed him diploma certificate and told him to prepare a resume and take it along with him. He then headed straight to the office of the company to meet with the personnel manager.

The company was Institute of Information Services or the IIS. When he reached the office, he found at least thirty candidates waiting for their turn to be called in for an interview. He handed over his resume to the receptionist and took a seat in the waiting area. He did not know the exact details of the job opening and was puzzled what would he reply when asked. He thought he should have asked his manager about this before coming here. He was appearing for an interview for the first time. The only thought that crossed his mind was, "let me give it my best and see what happens."

He had a very successful interview with the personnel manager. He was appointed to the post of executive and was required to join in a week's time. He came to know he had to undergo induction training for 30 days. Upon completion, he could be transferred to any of the offices in India. Krishna was on cloud nine. He could not believe how his life had changed. He had come to the institute to collect his certificate and that he has now had a job with no struggle.

A FACULTY

Krishna came into the office of the Institute of Information Services at Salt Lake. The Salt Lake office was the training center for employees. He met with the manager there and handed over the letter from the personnel manager to him. His training would begin from today.

Krishna left the manager's office and went to the training room. He saw ten trainees seated in the room. He realized that he was one among the hundred candidates interviewed over the last week. Surprisingly, only a dozen of them were here for training. He felt honored to be here. The training began with presentation skills, and he had the opportunity to learn from his trainer, and he gave his best.

On the third day at the office, he came to know that he had to undergo an advanced level of training. To do this, he had to go to Delhi, the head office of IIS. Krishna was exhilarated hearing the news. He wanted to know how many of them were going to Delhi. At the end of the day, the news came in. There were five trainees including him who were to go to Delhi in 2 days' time. The manager handed over the train ticket and wished them good luck.

Krishna went home that day very happy knowing that this opportunity would catapult his career. Two days later, Krishna with four of his colleagues made the train journey from Kolkata to New Delhi. On reaching New Delhi railway station, he called the head office and informed them of their arrival. The office informed him that he needed to wait in the waiting room, and someone would meet him in an hour's time. Krishna and his colleagues shifted to the waiting room. After waiting for over forty-five minutes, a middle-aged gentleman arrived at the waiting room. He introduced himself as Mr. Aggarwal from the head office.

"Where do we go from here?"

"We will go straight to the training center. All of you will reside with me."

"You will train us sir?" asked Krishna inquisitively.

"Yes! I am your trainer and manager for rest of your training period."

Everyone kept silent and picked up their bags and followed Mr. Aggarwal out of the railway station to a van and drove off to the training center. Krishna had not been to Delhi before. He watched through the window as they traveled across Delhi.

"Where are we going, sir?"

"Gurgaon."

"Where is Gurgaon?"

"It is on the outskirts of Delhi. That is where the training center is."

"How long will it take to reach there?"

"We should be there within an hour or two."

After traveling for over an hour and a half, the van halted in front of a large two-storied house; this must be a residence of a high-ranking officer. The residence had a security guard stationed in front of the gate. Krishna thought this must be the house of the managing director.

"Get out, we have reached," said Mr. Aggarwal standing in front of the gate.

Krishna looked at the building in front of him in amazement. He quickly picked up the bag and disembarked the van and walked along with Mr. Aggarwal into the building. A concrete pathway led to the main door. On the either side of the pathway, soft green lawn perfectly cut and flower bed around it. As they entered through the main door, into a spacious hall, on the left of the hall was the dining area with four tables and hot steaming food waiting for them. On the right, two rows of dining table set neatly placed were waiting for the guests.

Mr. Aggarwal told the trainees to occupy a bed in any of the rooms on the first floor. The training would start at 8 a.m. following day. It was noon when they came to the training center, and lunch was ready to be served. Krishna and his colleagues went up the staircase to the first floor. There were five rooms on the first floor. Each room had five beds with fresh white bed sheets and blankets neatly placed at one end. Krishna had a look at all the rooms and selected the room which opened to the balcony from where he could see the lawn down below. By evening, teams of trainees arrived from Delhi, Lucknow, Hyderabad, and Madras who occupied the rest of the rooms.

The training he was to receive was to be a trainer. He had to undergo training on presentation skills, question handling, and class control. He was to become a faculty in the institute. Every day, the training would commence at sharp 8 a.m. and end at 8 p.m. It was an intensive training program. He would be extremely exhausted at the end of the day. After the training had ended, he had to complete his assignments for the day. He had to work long hours working on the computer till late night as he had to make a presentation the following day.

On one such day, Mr. Aggarwal was explaining a computer programming algorithm. He said, "There is only one algorithm for this problem."

"I think there is another approach, I can do it," replied Krishna.

"If there is one, show me at tea break," remarked Mr. Aggarwal.

At the tea break, Krishna rushed to the computer and started working on the problem with a different approach which he had already written on his notepad. After two tries, he could solve it. He rushed to Mr. Aggarwal and requested him to come to his computer and check it out. Mr. Aggarwal had gone through his code before he ran the computer program. "Good logic, Krishna! Well done!"

A fortnight had passed. One day, Mr. Aggarwal informed the trainees that a special assignment was planned for successful presentation by the trainees to the managing director, a pet project of the managing director.

After preparation for a day, Krishna made his presentation to the managing director and Mr. Aggarwal. He was happy that his presentation went well. The competition was tough. He was competing with experienced teachers from Delhi and Hyderabad. Krishna waited with bated breath. At the end of the presentation by all trainees to the managing director, Mr. Aggarwal announced a list of seven trainees selected for the project, and Krishna was one among them. He would get a raise of fifteen hundred rupees with immediate effect.

Hearing this, Krishna was elated. He had to undergo a one-week specialized training for the project. He finally came to know more about the project. He became a faculty in a government-run fully residential school. He had to be independent as there would be no one to guide him. He received training to handle all situations independently in this training. He learned everything he could in these few days. An immense challenge for him as he could not afford to fail. He not only had to conduct classes for students but also the hands-on practical sessions as well. He had to conduct himself in a manner such that the image of the company gets a boost, and the company expected more schools to sign up. He had a huge responsibility on his shoulders.

Krishna was ready for his placement to a school of Navodaya Vidyalaya. These schools are called Jawahar Navodaya Vidyalayas. More information about his school came in. He had to go to a remote village and live there and teach students. These schools are managed by the Department of Human Resources, Government of India. It was a privilege to be given the opportunity to teach here. Each district of a state had only one school, and not all states or districts had them. The project had been a dream project of then the Prime Minister, Rajiv Gandhi. Krishna also came to know that teachers who joined these schools are the best the nation had ever produced. Teachers came here on deputation from the "Kendriya Vidyalaya Sangathan" or Central School. He received training to teach up to Plus-2 level. Two years ago, he was a Plus-2 student himself, but now he was to be a teacher in a school.

The following day, Krishna attended a conference at the Navodaya Vidyalaya Samiti headquarters. He came here with his six other colleagues and the managing director. They were to represent the company in seven schools across India.

Krishna and his colleagues assembled in the conference room, and principals of the schools walked in. The meeting commenced. The managing director of IIS introduced them to the Samiti secretary and the principals. Krishna was to go to Jawahar Navodaya Vidyalaya, Hadagarh, a remote village in rural Orissa.

"Good morning, I am Dr. D. K. Dasmahapatra from JNV, Hadagarh."

"Good morning sir, Krishna Mitra from IIS."

"You are Bengali, good to know you. Do you speak Oriya?"

"Yes sir, I have lived in Orissa all my life."

"Good to have you as our computer teacher."

"Thank you, sir."

"We leave tomorrow."

"Yes, sir. The train is at 2 p.m. at Hazrat Nizamuddin railway station. I will take computer systems along with me to the school."

"How will you take them?"

"Book them in the luggage van."

"Okay, that's good. I have another meeting scheduled for tomorrow. We will meet at the Hazrat Nizamuddin railway station. See you there."

The following day, Krishna left Delhi for his onward journey to his school in Orissa. Krishna did not have any idea about the school and its location. All that matters most, he was a faculty in a reputed school in the country.

LAW OF THE JUNGLE

Krishna disembarked from the train at Cuttack railway station. He went straight to the luggage van to get the computer systems. He arranged a porter to carry them to the luggage office for clearance. The principal also joined at the railway station. They hired a taxi to take them all the way to the school. The taxi traveled along the highway and Krishna could see the vast expanse of paddy fields and farmers tilling the land and sowing the seedlings and singing songs as the put the seedlings manually into the water-filled paddy fields. The taxi took a sudden right turn onto the dusty road along the mountain range. The sun was setting beyond the mountain. There were no street lights along the road. The road was narrow, winding, and dusty. They had entered the forest. Krishna saw large trees with thick foliage on either side of the road. The sun had set, and the view was pitch-dark. The light from the headlights of the taxi fell on the trees along the side of the road. The taxi suddenly stopped in the middle of the road, and the driver switched off the headlights.

Krishna asked, "What happened?"
"A herd of elephants is crossing the road," replied the driver.

They halted there for fifteen minutes and then the driver started the engine and switched on the headlights again. They drove through the forest for fifteen minutes and stopped at a barricade manned by a forest guard. The forest guard came in closer to the car and peeped in. He saluted the principal and then opened the barricade for the car to pass through.

"We have reached." Krishna looked around. He could hardly see anything. It was pitch-black, only a twinkling light from a small house a few meters away.

"The school is closed for vacation, will reopen on Monday. Stay here. I will get the keys to the office." And he walked away in the dark into the school.

He could hear the principal calling out to get the keys to the office. He heard footsteps rushing through. He could barely see a few meters ahead of him. The darkness had engulfed him. The man opened the door of the principal's office and switched on the lights. An intense beam of light tearing across the darkness fell on his feet. His pupils dilated to adjust the sudden light around him; he could see much better. He stood before a veranda with four rooms side by side. At the extreme right was the principal's office. Lights switched on in the principal's office lit up the night sky. The principal went into the office. The man rushed to him, picked up all the boxes one by one and kept it in the principal's office.

The principal introduced Krishna to the Hindi teacher, Mr. Ajay Bhardwaj. Mr. Bhardwaj was a very jovial person. He welcomed Krishna to his home. He was to share the house with Mr. Bhardwaj. Krishna moved his belonging to a room and settled down.

"Where are you from Krishna?"

"I am from Kolkata."

"Good to have a Bengali as a friend. I love Bengali. It is a very sweet language."

"How long have you been here?"

"Oh! Three years now. I am from Gorakhpur."

"Three years! A long time! How often do you meet your family?"

"Only in summer vacations. Last summer, I went home. I have a 5-year-old son. He will be going to school soon. What about you? Are you married?"

"No sir, I am not. Too young to be."

"How old are you?"

"Twenty."

"We have pretty ladies here. You will find someone to marry."

"No plans yet."

"Come, it is dinner time. Let's go to the dining hall."

Krishna accompanied Mr. Bhardwaj to the dining hall. On the way, they met with students who greeted them. Seeing Krishna, the students discussed among themselves that a new teacher had come to the school. The dining hall was very large, with rows of tables and benches with a sitting capacity of over three hundred. The kitchen and the storeroom were on the left. Cooks were making chapattis on firewood in an open furnace. After a long time, he saw firewood used in a kitchen. It reminded him of his childhood days where he went out in the forest with his family for a picnic. For Krishna, it was picnic every day, henceforth. This was fun.

The following morning, Krishna was out for a morning walk with Mr. Bhardwaj. He was amidst the mountain range with thick jungle spanning from east to west and a winding gravel road leading to a valley. The school was in a valley, a small hamlet. Mango groves at one end and a stream flowing through the valley. The school premises had no boundary wall. Two rows of quarters on either side of the road and a huge playground behind it. A little walk uphill was the school building.

"What is this place? It does not look like a school campus."

"Yes, this is a township of Irrigation Department. There is a dam up there. Construction workers lived here, most of the houses are now vacant, and we have the school up and running."

"Oh, I love it. Such a calm and quiet place."

"Come, I will show you around. We will go to the dam."

They walked uphill past the school building onto a straight road going towards the dam. On the left, small huts on the foothills of the mountain. After walking a mile, they reached the top of the hill; behold, the dam before them. The dam was small, and vast span of blue water held by the dam. A small building at this end of the dam, a guest house for the Forest Department. Krishna realized that the stream that he saw some time back was downstream of the river.

"City people cannot stay here for long, too lonely place, nothing to do."

"I like it. I will stay here."

"Time will tell."

Krishna noticed two armed men with bows and arrows approaching him.

"Who are they?"

"Hunters, off to the forest for hunting."

"What will they hunt?"

"Deer."

"Is deer meat tasty?"

"I presume so; the villagers love it."

"Can I go with them?"

"No, you should not! You are from a city. You will not be able to withstand their rugged lifestyle. It is not advisable, wild animals in the jungle; elephants and tigers."

"Oh, tigers too!"

"Did you see elephants."

"Presumably, on my way here last night."

In the afternoon, Krishna was at the school to meet the principal at his office. He had to convert a classroom to a computer lab. He got the services of the school electrician and had the wiring done. He found some old tables and benches in the store and placed them in his computer lab. He opened the boxes of computer systems and assembled them one by one. He tested all the computer systems, and they were working fine. The last box contained books for distribution to the students. He assembled them in one corner of the room. The principal sent a teacher's table and a chair. Finally, his computer lab was ready that very day up and running.

The following Monday, the school, reopened after the winter vacation. All students assembled at the prayer hall. The principal introduced him as the computer teacher from Delhi. Krishna had begun his new role as a school teacher.

Krishna was very warm and loving with his students and colleagues. Every class he went to, he found students were very eager to learn computers from him and were asking many questions which he gladly answered. He had built a very good rapport with all the students within a day or two. Students used to follow him wherever he went. Someone or the other would come up to him talk to him whenever they saw him alone. Krishna was motivated to do more.

Encouraged by the participation of the students, Krishna announced a quiz competition for the students. He asked students of each class to give names of four students as a team. He got three teams from each class. The list was put up on the notice board. The competition was held that weekend. The event turned out to be very successful. He sent all the names of the students to IIS. After about fifteen days, IIS sent him the participation certificate along with a letter of appreciation from the managing director.

Another week had just passed; the principal informed that the director of Jawahar Navodaya Vidyalaya would visit the school next week. He requested all the teachers to be ready for inspection.

The day had come. The director was visiting the school. The principal appraised the director of the sincere efforts of Krishna to bring about awareness of computer education among the students. The director was very pleased. At the end of the day, he called upon Krishna to the principal's office.

"I like your attitude. You have motivated the students to learn computers. Every student that I talked to wanted to be a computer teacher. Congratulations, keep up the good work."

He took out his letterhead and wrote down the letter of appreciation to IIS and handed over to Krishna. He was on cloud nine. He could not believe what he received. He showed the letter to his dear friend, Mr. Bharadwaj.

"You know Krishna; no one has been able to satisfy the director today. He was furious with us, but today, he gave you an appreciation letter! I never knew he was a generous person."

Months had passed, one day Krishna was in class VIII. He heard a large number of birds chirping in the trees and flying away, and then he heard small animals hither and thither among the bushes nearby. He came out of the classroom and walked towards the main gate to the road leading to the dam. Then an abrupt silence, time stood still.

"Come back, Krishna," said the principal who saw Krishna walking out of the gate.

"What happened, sir? What is going on?"

"A tiger is on the prowl. Come back to school. It is not safe out there. Come back now."

Krishna turned back to the school, and the security closed the gate.

Krishna turned out to be a very passionate teacher. He conducted many more extracurricular activities in the school. He formed a computer club with his students. He took out monthly magazines prepared by the students to showcase the creative talents of the students. He had conquered their hearts and minds. He had become a very popular teacher among his students. All loved him, students and staff, alike.

Krishna did not realize how quickly one year had passed. As the year was coming to an end, the date of annual function of the school was declared. It was to be the last working day of the school.

Mr. Bharadwaj, the Hindi teacher, had just started writing a script of a Hindi play. He called upon Krishna to his room. He read the first act of the script to him with pride. The play was with abstract characters such as mother earth, hunger, and corruption, etc. He asked Krishna for his opinion of the script.

"What do you say, Krishna! Won't it be interesting?"

"Yes, it will be a blockbuster. It should turn out to be captivating. How many acts are there in the play?"

"There are three acts. I want you to direct the play."

"Oh, no! I have never done it before."

"There is always a first time."

"No, no! I am not capable of direction."

"You are from the land of Tagore, Vivekananda, and Ramakrishna. I firmly believe you can do it."

Krishna had no choice, but to accept the challenge given to him by Mr. Bharadwaj.

Krishna chose the cast from among his students of his computer club. Mr. Bharadwaj continued writing the script every day. He used to read the script at late evening to Krishna and ask Krishna to think about it for the direction the next day. Krishna had to train the students on dialogue delivery. They practiced the play as the play was being written act after act. After writing of the play was complete, Krishna went on with his students under the guidance of Mr. Bharadwaj to practice the play day after day.

It was the last working day of school. The annual function was to be held today. The parents of children started to arrive. Although it was a very busy day for the students, they were very happy to meet with their parents. A letter from the post office was delivered to him. It was from IIS sent by the personnel manager. He opened the letter. He was shocked to read the mail. He was transferred to Delhi with immediate effect. This news devastated him. He informed the principal of the same.

"I am very sorry to hear that. What are you going to do now?"

"I have to leave immediately. I will make a brief stopover at Kolkata and then proceed to Delhi."

The function started at 4 p.m. The chief guest was the district forest officer who inaugurated the function. The news of Krishna of his transfer spread like wildfire. The atmosphere became very somber. Krishna met with his student artists and said them to be strong and to do whatever best they can. Today is their day. Their parents were here. They had to make them proud of them. Krishna quietly stood at one end of the auditorium watching the function.

The students performed an English play, Hindi play, and Oriya play. The Hindi play was an instantaneous hit. The principal, staff, and parents congratulated him.

The school closed for winter vacation. The next day, Krishna returned to home; a year after he had been to Delhi. He met with James at his home. James had completed his computer course and was awaiting placement. James mother served them tea. As Krishna sipped the tea, James's mother said, "I have an important matter to discuss."

"Yes, of course."

"How was your school?"

"Fantastic! I had a good time."

"Krishna, I want you to guide James so that he can get a job at IIS."

"There is a possibility he will have to go to Delhi."

"I know that. I will let him go."

"Okay, I will take him to our office tomorrow. I am leaving for Delhi at night."

Krishna took James to his Kolkata office and introduced him to the manager. James went through the interview process that very day. That night, Krishna went back to Delhi. He went to the training center at Gurgaon.

While he was in Gurgaon, he received a call from James informing him that he got the job. He was now undergoing training at Kolkata office. Krishna wrote a letter congratulating James his achievement.

TUSSI GREAT HO

After a week's stay at Gurgaon, Krishna received a call from the head office. The personnel manager had called him to come to the office the following day. He realized that this meeting was to discuss his next assignment. He traveled to Delhi to the IIS head office. He met with Mr. Aggarwal, very pleased with his performance at JNV Hadagarh. Mr. Aggarwal explained to him that the managing director wanted him back, so he was called back. Krishna was relieved. He then met with the personnel manager at his cubicle.

"Welcome back, Krishna. How was your stay at JNV Hadagarh?"

"A quiet and peaceful place."

"We here at the head office are very pleased with you."

"Thank you very much!"

"We have decided to promote you. You will be going to Punjab. Are you willing to go?"

"Yes, sir."

"You are aware of Punjab, right?"

"Yes, I read it in a newspaper."

"Would you like to talk to your parents?"

"Where will I be posted?"

"Jalandhar."

"I will go. I will inform my parents when I reach Jalandhar."

"That's the spirit. Fantastic! That's what I expected. I had given this offer to two others who declined."

"You will leave tomorrow. I will get your train ticket. Please collect it before you leave."

"Thank you, sir."

"Good luck to you."

Krishna unaware of the ground reality and had just accepted whatever offered to him. He had some information about Punjab. Stray incidents of killing by terrorists were periodically reported in newspapers. All that he understood was that these terrorist groups informed through media, of the people on their hit list and then targeted them specifically. He thought it was not a threat to him. People continue to live there, and there was no mass exodus. Therefore, he was ready to go to Punjab. If he could live a year in a jungle, he could be in Punjab as well. He was going to a city, not the jungle anymore.

The following day, he went to New Delhi railway station and took a train to Jalandhar. As he traveled through the streets of Jalandhar, he saw army patrolling the streets. He could also see bunkers built at various intersections of roads, manned by fully armed army soldiers who were ready to fire at anyone suspicious. He did not expect this. His assessment of the situation was entirely wrong.

He was at IIS Jalandhar early morning, a two-storied building similar to that of the training center at Gurgaon. He rang the doorbell at the gate. The caretaker, Raju, came running and opened the lock of the gate. Raju picked the baggage took him straight to the first floor. He opened the keys to the room and placed his baggage. The first floor had two rooms and a kitchen. No one around except Raju. "This is you room, *Sirjee*. I made it ready last night. I will get some tea for you. What would you like for breakfast?" "*Parathas*," replied Krishna.

Krishna came down to the ground floor to have a look. The institute premises comprised of a manager's office, two classrooms, and a computer lab on the ground floor. The office opens at 9 o'clock.

At around 9:30 a.m., he came down to meet with the manager, Sukhbir Singh. He was in his late twenties, 6 feet 2 inches tall, a broad chest, handsome gentleman with a big smile. He wore a neatly tied turban. He was a Sikh. All Sikh males are required to wear a turban, keep mustache and beard as a part of their faith. Krishna introduced himself to Sukhbir Singh and handed over the transfer order to him. Sukhbir Singh inquired about his last posting with IIS. Krishna shared his experience in a school in a deep forest. He was here to assist Sukhbir Singh and conduct the training programs of the institute. Sukhbir Singh introduced Krishna to Rajesh. Rajesh was very fair, an average-built gentleman with a goatee. He also met with Ranveer Singh, a faculty member at a school nearby.

In a few hours, Sukhbir Singh called upon Krishna and gave him his class schedule. He had to conduct professional training program at the institute. He had a week's time to prepare himself to conduct the classes. He mentioned that the batch was special, and Rajesh would not be able to handle it. Krishna gladly took over the new batch. He began to prepare to teach his students. Professional training was new to him. He received the list of students in his class, and he went through their background. To his utter surprise, he found that two of his students, Namita and Yamini were studying MBA. Lt. Col Dilbarg Singh, Col. Raghuveer Singh and Maj. Rana Malhotra were from the Indian Army. Mr. Praveen Mehra was the CEO and MD of Mehra Group of Industries, and Tamanna joined her father's business, a prominent hotelier. The rest seven were college students.

Krishna had to teach computer programming to this diverse group of students. He was a bit nervous. He had no experience of teaching students older than him. He began intensive preparations to make a debut class. On the day of his first class, he used all the skills he had learned in his training. It was an awesome experience for all his students. Col. Raghuveer Singh was very impressed. He met with Sukhbir Singh and requested that Krishna should continue until the end of the program and not to replace him until completion. Mr. Mehra requested for a special coaching from him as he had a specific need at his workplace which he wanted to address immediately.

Three months had passed; Krishna had kept himself very busy with his students. He kept himself occupied by taking classes during the morning hours. He used to be free by the evening. Evenings, he devoted his time towards marketing activities. He made follow-up visits to prospect's homes and talked to their parents, answered their queries and had them enrolled. He also made follow-up calls regularly. His efforts started to bear fruits. He had achieved a maximum number of enrollments in comparison to last three to four months. Sukhbir Singh was so pleased that he threw a party for Krishna. All the staffs attended the party and congratulated Krishna for his efforts. The IIS head office also took cognizance and promoted him to the post of assistant manager. Col. Raghuveer Singh was delighted to hear about Krishna's promotion.

Suddenly, the terrorists started to target innocent civilians across the city. They also sent messages to blow up vital installations in the city if their demands were not met. A dawn-to-dusk curfew imposed for three days. After the curfew had been lifted, the army patrolled every nook and corner of the major roads and vital installations in the city. Army sent artillery jeeps, fitted with heavy machine guns and cannon; which were followed by armored vans patrolling the streets. The black cat commando units were called in to aid with patrolling. Army along and the police force jointly put barricades at every junction in the city. People were frisked regularly at these junctions and asked to carry IDs. It is very unsafe to venture out in the streets. All schools and colleges had declared holidays, and shopkeepers downed their shutters before sunset. No one wanted to risk their life to remain on the streets after 7 p.m.

Krishna now realized the gravity of the situation as it unfolded before him. He remained in the institute and did not venture out after sunset. This situation waxed and waned for over two months. Extensive combing operations had been conducted jointly by the police force and the Army. The Army was able to eliminate the key terrorist commanders. Peace returned, and the city started limping back to normalcy.

Krishna was in his room on the first floor. He was resting after an exhaustive day at the office. Rajesh came to meet him in his room.

"I want to talk to you. It is private."

"What can I do for you?"

"I love Namita dearly. I cannot live without her."

"Go, talk to her."

"I tried, but could not express my feelings."

"What do you expect from me?"

"Namita is your student. She will listen to you. Please, please help me out."

"Does Namita know about your feelings?"

"Yes, I presume."

"Okay, I will talk to her."

"Thank you, you are an angel."

The following day, Krishna went up to Namita. She was in the computer lab working on her assignments. He asked her to meet with him after she had completed her assignments. She met with Krishna at his office.

"What is your opinion about Rajesh?"

"Rajesh sir is a good teacher. Sir, are you going to hand over our batch to him?"

"No, he loves you very much. He cannot live without you."

Namita put her head down and whispered, "I know that."

"Do you love him?"

"Yes, I do."

"Good, he is waiting for you on the first floor."

Namita left the office room and rushed to the first floor where Rajesh was waiting for her nervously. Rajesh and Namita had found each other. Another feather in Krishna's cap, made two hearts meet.

Several months had passed; Krishna was seated in the office the phone rang. The call came from head office. He was asked to come to Delhi immediately and bring along with him the collection register of the center. Krishna had no idea why the head office had asked for the register. He rushed to Delhi the following day and then to the training center at Gurgaon. He reached Gurgaon late in the evening. An emergency meeting was going on at the training center. All the branch managers of IIS were attending the meeting. He joined the meeting. He had to make a presentation of the collections of the last one year. After the end of his presentation, he came to know that Jalandhar had the highest collections. The managing director and senior management staff congratulated him for his efforts. Sukhbir Singh's request for a transfer to Chandigarh, his hometown, was accepted. The management decided to promote Krishna to the post of manager.

After his return from Delhi, he informed the all the staff members that Sukhbir Singh had been transferred to Chandigarh, and now he was the Manager. All his students were very pleased with the news. Col. Raghuveer Singh congratulated him and invited him to his residence for a private celebration.

The following day, Rajesh was with Krishna in his cabin. "I want to quit the job."

"Why? You are doing so well."

"I want to start my business."

"Which business?"

"I will start a training center."

"That's wonderful. When do you plan to launch it?"

"I have finalized a place at Model Town. The interior work has already started. Namita is by my side. She is helping me to realize my dream."

"I am so happy for you Rajesh. You have made a very wise decision."

Krishna was in constant touch with Rajesh. He used to visit the Rajesh's training center and guide him with the layout design of the institute. He also helped Rajesh to design his course curriculum and shared with him marketing and follow-up strategies that he followed at IIS. Rajesh and Namita launched their training institute in a month's time. Krishna was the guest of honor at the inauguration ceremony of their center. Rajesh's parents and Namita's parents met with him for the first time. They thanked him for all his support and mentorship.

THE REALIZATION

Krishna had been managing the institute single-handedly for all these months. Rajesh had settled with his new institute and was doing well. He found it very difficult to manage the institute all by himself. He, therefore, made a request to the head office for a faculty member to support him. The personnel manager at the head office accepted and would send someone soon.

A week later, Krishna received a call from the personnel manager that James had been requested to go to Jalandhar. He was overjoyed to hear the news. James had been working at the Kolkata office since he had joined IIS. Krishna called James and informed him that he had to come to Jalandhar. James was very happy to be with his dearest friend, Krishna. He immediately accepted the transfer to Jalandhar and within two days' time he was on his way.

The day James arrived at Jalandhar, Krishna went to the railway station to receive him. He had to wait at the railway station as the train was delayed by 30 minutes. He met with James at the platform where the train had just arrived. They hugged each other and were very happy to see a dear friend. Krishna and James came to the institute. Raju greeted them at the gate of the institute. Raju picked up the baggage and carried them to the room, adjacent to Krishna's room on the first floor.

"This is your room. I am at the next door to you."

"Thank you so much, Krishna."

"Raju has prepared this room for you. Hope you will like it."

"Great. I love it. Thank you, Raju."

"The breakfast will be served in ten minutes. Please get ready."

Raju rushed to the kitchen to prepare the breakfast. After the breakfast, Krishna showed James around his training center and introduced him to the students of the center. Krishna handed over to James the batches Rajesh used to teach. James was a dedicated teacher and taught his students with a lot of zeal and enthusiasm. His students loved the way he taught.

Krishna had been in Jalandhar for over a year now. He had received multiple letters from his mother requesting him to come home. He wrote back that he was unable to go this year, but would surely make it in February next year. Krishna planned to train James to manage the center only then he would be able to go on leave to visit his parents. James was also in touch with Krishna's parents and kept them abreast of the situation in Jalandhar.

Six months had gone by, Rajesh and Namita had been able to run their institute successfully. Namita's father had been financially supporting his daughter's business venture from the start. They were now planning to take their relationship to the next level. Rajesh's parents had sent the proposal to Namita's parents about their marriage. Namita's parents gladly accepted their proposal. A grand party organized for their engagement. Krishna along with James and his colleagues attended the party. At the engagement party, the parents announced the date of marriage. They were to get married on November 12th.

Just about a week before marriage Rajesh and Namita came to IIS and invited Krishna and his colleagues to their marriage. Rajesh had also invited few of his students from the institute. Namita had also made sure her dear friend, Yamini, came to her wedding. The marriage was to take place in Faridkot. Krishna decided to attend the marriage ceremony. James and Ranveer joined him. Ranveer would drive them to Faridkot. They decided to leave the night before. Rajesh also invited Sukhbir Singh, and he would come directly to Faridkot.

On the day of departure, at 10 p.m., Ranveer brought his vehicle to the institute, an open Gypsy. A Gypsy is similar to a Jeep Wrangler. Krishna and James hopped on to it. They also picked up three of the students accompanying them and began their journey to Faridkot. Winter nights are very chilly. They covered themselves with heavy woolen blankets to protect themselves in the cold winter night. As they drove by, they came across multiple checkpoints in the city where Ranveer slowed down and was allowed to pass through. After an hour's drive, they reached the highway to Faridkot.

As soon as, they were on the highway; Ranveer hit the gas pedal. The Gypsy was now cruising at the speed of 100 to 120 kilometers per hour. After over a forty-minute drive, suddenly, Ranveer slowed down again; they approached a checkpoint in the middle of nowhere. Krishna saw an armed soldier with sophisticated weapons asking them to halt. Ranveer stopped the Gypsy at the side of the road. A soldier came close to them and lit a flashlight on their faces and then asked to stop the engine. Ranveer obliged. Another soldier approached them; he asked all of them to get out of the vehicle one by one and stand in a queue ten feet away. The soldier frisked them one by one. A sniffer dog was brought in to check the vehicle. The soldiers wanted to know their source and destination. Ranveer replied they were going to Faridkot to attend a wedding. The soldiers were not convinced and asked to meet with the officer-in-charge.

Ranveer said, "Gypsy is a vehicle of choice for the militants because of its speed and agility."
"Guys be here, I will go and meet the officer," said Krishna. As he entered the tent of the officer-in-charge, he saw Major Rana Malhotra in conversation with four of his men.
"Hi, Major Rana."
"Sir, you are here? Where are you going?"
"We are all going to Faridkot to attend Rajesh and Namita's wedding."

He called upon his men and instructed them to see off Krishna to the Gypsy. He also mentioned that he was sending a patrol vehicle ahead of their Gypsy to ensure safe journey through his territory.

Krishna came back to the Gypsy and said, "We can go now. A patrol van will lead us through."

Ranveer was amazed and said, "Tussi great ho."
"Oye, that was Major Rana Malhotra, yaar!" replied Krishna.

They reached Faridkot at in the early hours of the morning. It was around 3 a.m., still dark. Rajesh came out and greeted them. He led them to a building in the marriage hall complex. The building was a two-storied building. The main door leads to a courtyard at the center. There were several rooms all around. Krishna, James, and Ranveer occupied one of the rooms on the ground floor, and the students were in the adjacent room. It was time to rest for a while after a hectic journey in the cold, chilly night.

It was a cold winter morning; the sun was not visible. A dense fog had arisen, which made it impossible to see beyond twenty feet. Krishna had woken up, decided to stroll around the place. He walked out of the complex along the pavement. He saw two storied houses all along the road

Each house had a staircase, which went from the side of the house to the first floor; and opened to a large open space. There were two rooms in the far end of the house. Almost all houses had the similar design. He stopped at a small shop. The owner was selling milk and tea and *jalebi*. *Jalebi* is dessert a made by deep-frying a wheat flour batter in pretzel or circular shapes, which then soaked in sugar syrup.

The owner had a large flat-bottomed cooking pot placed over a gas stove and steaming milk served in a large tumbler of approximately 10 inches in height tapering at the bottom. Krishna had not seen such large tumblers used before. He could not resist himself and purchased a hot glass of milk and 200 grams of *jalebi*. Here *jalebis* were sold as per weight and not as a unit. He relished it thoroughly as he sat on a stool in front of the roadside stall.

He then went back to the room and joined James who had just woken up. Many family members of Namita came and introduced themselves to Krishna. Yamini had also arrived in the morning and joined with Namita at her residence. By afternoon, Sukhbir Singh also arrived from Chandigarh. Sukhbir Singh, Ranveer, James and Krishna sat in the courtyard in front of their room and were in conversation with few other guests. Suddenly, James pulled Krishna aside.

"I presume, I saw Paro."

"What! Where did you see her?"

"Just a while ago, few ladies walked out of this building, one of them was Paro."

"No way! How can she be here?" Krishna remarked in amazement.

"Just check," replied James.

Krishna ran out of the building. He looked around for a group of ladies. He saw a group of ladies walking briskly away from the marriage hall complex. He ran toward them and crossed them and halted to have a look. He could not find Paro. He asked pardon and walked briskly toward the marriage hall. He saw Paro walking down the steps.

"Paro! Oh My God! What a pleasant surprise!" Paro stood there with her eyes wide open and tears rolled down her cheek.

"Krishna! You! Here? You have changed a lot!"

"I came to Rajesh and Namita's wedding."

"How do you know Rajesh?"

"Rajesh was my colleague in Jalandhar and Namita, my student."

"Oh, you are famous."

"Famous! Not really! Who invited you?"

"Namita is my distant cousin."

"I waited all my life to see you."

"Please let me go."

"No, you cannot leave just like that. What is wrong with you? We just met after so many years."

"You never replied to my letter."

"I am sorry, Paro."

"You know what I went through. Let me go now."

Krishna held Paro's wrist and said, "I love you, Paro. We can make a new beginning." Paro released the grip of Krishna over her wrist by releasing his fingers one by one.

"I am sorry Krishna, not in this life, we meet in the next. Promise me." and Paro walked away.

"Where is Paro?" asked James who came running.

"She just left me, yet again," replied Krishna and stood perplexed before the marriage hall.

James went after Paro. He saw Paro crying and walking away briskly; along the alley, towards the mustard fields. He rushed back to Krishna.

"Parmeet is going towards the mustard fields," shouted James.

"She is going towards the canal," said Ranveer who had rushed there with Sukhbir Singh and few others.

Ranveer rushed towards his Gypsy and started the engine, turned it around and halted.

"Get in," said Ranveer.

Sukhbir Singh and James hopped in at the back of the Gypsy. Krishna took the seat in front. Ranveer drove out of the marriage hall complex through the alley and onto the narrow pebbled road across the mustard fields. He stopped next to a footbridge over the canal.

Paro stood at the center of the foot bridge looking at the blue water flowing furiously through the canal. She was about to jump into the canal. Krishna jumped out of the Gypsy and rushed to stop Paro from jumping into the canal. He grabbed her around her waist and pulled her away from the edge of the bridge. He slapped Paro very hard on her cheek. Paro fainted in his arms. Krishna lifted Paro with his two hands and brought her and laid her in the back seat of the Gypsy and sat next to her. Sukhbir Singh and James hopped in the Gypsy, and Ranveer drove them back to marriage hall complex.

Krishna picked up Paro again and took her inside the building into the courtyard. He put her in a cot lying there. Paro's mother noticed this and came rushing to nurse her daughter. Following this, Nimmi, Bhabhiji, and Paro's brother joined them.

Paro's mother asked, "Oh, God! What happened to my daughter."
"She has fainted. She was trying to jump off the bridge" said James. Paro's mother started to fan with her *dupatta*. Nimmi rushed to bring in a glass of water and handed over to Krishna.

Paro's mother looked at Krishna in amazement and asked: "Krishna! You are here!"
"We are invited to Rajesh and Namita's wedding."

"How do you know Rajesh?"

"I live in Jalandhar. He was my colleague. Namita was my student."

"Oh! I see."

She turned towards her son and said, "We would not have to see this day if you would not have put so much pressure on her."

"Mummy, this is not the time to talk about all this."

Krishna sprinkled water on Paro's face, and she slowly regained consciousness. Krishna lifted her and held her in a big bear hug. Paro started to cry aloud in his arms.

"Get them married," said her mother.

"Yes, mummy, we will do that," replied her brother. Everybody gave a round of applause.

"Uncle and aunt are coming," said James.

"My parents are coming! How do you know that?" said Krishna in astonishment.

"Your mother had called the office yesterday. They will come next week. It is a surprise for you."

"We will come to Jalandhar next week," said Paro's mother.

Paro was delighted to hear this. Her tears had dried out, and she stopped crying. Everyone was overjoyed and congratulated Krishna and Paro. Nimmi and Bhabhiji hugged her. Bhabhiji said, "I had told you, everything will become okay, have faith in God."

Namita's parents came to know and were delighted that Paro and Krishna were in love with each other, but fate took them apart. Namita's mother shared about the role of

Krishna in the lives of Rajesh and Namita. Namita's father promised that he would come along with them to meet Krishna's parents when they visit him.

A week later, Krishna parents came to Jalandhar. Krishna was waiting for this day for a very long time. Krishna informed his mother about Paro and how he happened to meet her at Rajesh and Namita's wedding. Krishna's mother knew about Paro from James. James had told her about Paro when he used to visit them frequently while Krishna was away in Orissa.

Krishna's parents thus gladly accepted his choice and blessed him. Namita's parents along with Paro, Paro's mother, Nimmi, Bhabhiji and her brother visited them that evening. Paro was accepted into their family, and their marriage was to be decided soon after Krishna's parents returned home from their trip.

Krishna and Paro were married in the following month. He had invited all his colleagues from the institute. James was the best man at the wedding. Rajesh and Namita also attended the wedding. Ranveer, Sukhbir Singh, Col. Raghuveer Singh, and Major Rana Malhotra also attended the wedding and blessed the couple. Partha and Riya also attended the wedding. He had also invited all of his college friends. Manoj and Anita, Joy, Pinky, Dipti, Sandeep, David, Ravi and Indrani had been there to witness the wedding of their dearest friends.

This is the story of Krishna and his journey of life. Krishna was a self-made man. He had his dreams. He chased his dreams in spite of fear; the fear of failures. He had his failures along the way. He persisted and strived ahead. He learned very quickly from his mistakes. He believed in love. He loved people around him. Anyone who came in contact with him admired his selflessness. Thus, he was surrounded by many friends and well-wishers. He was abundant in giving. He loved his friends and was always there for them. He gave more and thus he received in abundance when he needed the most. Giving is much more fulfilling than receiving.

About the Author

The author began his career in the IT training industry. He has served reputed companies, such as NIIT and CMC Ltd. He was a faculty member in their institute. He had also been in IT consultant after that. He switched domain to his long lost love of medicine. He has been a Quality Analyst with Spheris India, CBay Systems(M*Modal) and MD Online and through them served reputed university hospitals and clinics in the United States of America working with medical records spanning over a decade. He is a certified trainer on completion of "Train The Trainer" certification by Success Resources – T. Harv Eker. An author by choice pens his first novel – *A Silent Shadow*, a fiction; picking up bits and pieces from his life.

****

Printed in the United States
By Bookmasters